THE EX I CAN'T FORGET

HOPE FORD

The Ex I Can't Forget © 2025 by Hope Ford

Editor: Kasi Alexander

Proofreader: Nicole Graf

Cover Design: Cormar Covers

Cover Model: Joel Ros

Cover Photographer: Jane Ashley Converse

CHAPTER 1
LOGAN

I can't keep putting it off.

I haven't been back in the office since the day I found out my business partner hired my ex-girlfriend. I've kept busy, taking on assignments that take me as far from Whiskey Run as I can get. But my business, Stronghold Security, won't survive with a boss that never comes in, so I'm going to have to face the music and walk into the office. Even if every time I look at Bree, my heart cracks a little wider. And even if seeing her that first day made me realize I'm not over her. Fuck, nowhere near it.

I look up at the new sign for the business. *Stronghold Security*. It's big, bold, and lit up on Main Street. Zach and I talked about the design, and I knew it was coming, but seeing it now really makes me feel that it's all coming together. He told me in an email last week that Bree had been working on it and it would be up this week. Hell, every email I get from him mentions something about Bree. There's no escaping her.

I get out of my truck and take a deep breath. It's still dark, and there's at least another hour before the sun rises, but Bree is already here. I had hoped to get here and go straight to my office and shut the door. Hell, I'd planned to stay there all day if it meant I could avoid her.

As I look into the big bay windows, I see her already stationed at her desk. She has her hair in curls, and it's hanging over her shoulders. My jaw tightens as I think about our time together. It was two years ago, but it might as well have been yesterday. We met in the produce section of some bodega in New York. I was on an assignment with the Ghost Team, and I was happy to be on a mission in the States instead of overseas. I remember looking up from the apples and there she was, reaching into a stand-up cooler for a drink on the top shelf. Her back was to me, and as my eyes traveled down her body, I knew in that instant that she was going to be mine. Her curvy body and luscious ass had me taking a step toward her, wanting to block her from the sight of any other men. I didn't know anything about her. Hell, I hadn't even seen her face, but I'd never reacted to a woman like this in my life, and I knew she was meant to be mine.

And when she turned and gave me an apologetic smile, asking me to reach something for her, I knew in that moment that I would go to the ends of the Earth for this woman. She's beautiful in a way that takes your breath away, and I felt like a fool as I just nodded and pulled out the drink she wanted. I held the bottle out to her, but I didn't let it go. I remember the urgency I felt, as if letting go meant she'd walk away from me and I'd never see her again.

"Hi," I stuttered.

She bit her plump lip, her smile widening. "Hi."

"Go to dinner with me."

I realized after I said it that it was more of a demand than a request, but she didn't even blink. It was almost as if she was feeling everything I was feeling. She looked down at her sweatshirt and leggings and then back up at me. "I can't go like this. I just got out of a workout class, and I should shower."

My legs almost buckled just thinking about her in the shower. I cleared my throat. "You look beautiful. And…"

I paused because I knew that the words that were about to come out of my mouth were too controlling, too possessive, just too much. Hell, I still didn't even know her name at that point, and I was about to tell her that there was no way I was leaving this store without her.

She lifted her chin at me curiously. "And what?"

I clenched the bottle in my hand to stop from reaching for her as the words tumbled from my lips. "And I don't want to let you out of my sight."

She blinked up at me, and I continued. "I figure you're not going to tell me where you live just yet… not until we know each other better. And I don't want to let you go until I know everything there is to know about you."

I fully expected her to walk away or even call the cops. We didn't even know each other. It was a big city, not like Whiskey Run, where everybody knows each other. She surprised me, though, and just shrugged. "There's a great Italian place just around the corner. Does that work for you?"

I let out a huge breath and nodded. "Yeah, that's perfect. Anything you want."

Her eyes lit up at that, and instantly I thought of all the things I wanted to do to her.

And as we walked to the counter so I could pay for our things, I knew that my life was about to be forever changed. I just didn't realize that it would include a broken heart that destroyed me.

I blink as if I'm shutting out the past and bringing myself into the now. I can do this. Hell, I have to. I firm my jaw and pull my shoulders back and walk into the office.

I have every intention to walk right past Bree without a glance. But I only get three steps into the room before she breaks the silence. "Good morning, Logan."

My heart does a shimmy in my chest just hearing her voice. It's soft and low, bringing back memories of the two of us in her bedroom. And even though I know I shouldn't, I lift my head and look into her eyes. I stop in my tracks. "What's wrong with you?"

She flinches at my tone but pulls herself together quickly. "Nothing is wrong with me."

I gesture to her face. "You look tired."

Her cheeks bloom red as she rolls her eyes. "Well, thank you for that, Logan. You look well-rested."

My first thought is she's lying because there's no way I look well-rested. Hell, I haven't slept through the night in the last three months. And second, she's clearly not going to tell me what's going on.

I put my hands on her desk and lean over her. "What's wrong with you? Are you sick?"

I wait for her reply. Bree was always sassy, and I'm expecting a zinger comeback, but instead she just shakes her head. "No, I'm not sick. I'm just not getting enough sleep."

Her answer angers me so much that there's no holding back. I stand up and shove a thumb in my chest. "You work for me. Don't let your night-time activities affect the job you're doing here because I'll fire you. I don't care what the contract says."

I blow past her to my office and slam the door shut behind me. My breaths are coming in rapid succession, and I lean my back against the door to try and pull myself together. I knew it would be hard seeing her again, but I wasn't prepared for this. Especially when she mentioned not getting enough sleep. It made me think back to all of our sleepless nights together, and the thought of her with another man now makes me crazy.

When my pulse comes back to normal, I open my eyes and look around. This is not the same office I walked out of three months ago. The boxes are gone, the walls are no longer bare, and there are blinds over the window. Tense, I walk around the room. There's a huge rug on the floor and a leather couch that I've never seen before along the far wall. I walk toward my desk, my eyes drawn to the framed images on the wall behind it. One is a family picture with my five brothers and sister and our mom and dad. Another is a photo of Zach and me on one of our many missions. There's a framed newspaper article about the medal of freedom I won five years ago. I stare at picture after picture, each one just as important and meaningful as the last, and it softens me in a way that I don't expect.

I walk over to my desk and sit down. There's a computer, a cup of pens, a stapler. Hell, everything I could possibly need. I look down at the notepad, and written in big, curly writing is a username and password. Looking around the room, I don't have to question who did all this. I know it was Bree, and that fact hits me right in the chest. I want to hate her. Hell, she cheated on me. I thought we were in love, and while I was planning on asking her to marry me, she was seeing another man.

She can do all the nice things, but none of it is going to make up for what she did to me… to us. Nothing.

There's no way I can forget or forgive her. That moment has replayed in my head for two years now. Her with another man, leaning in to kiss him right on the lips as if what we had meant nothing to her.

No, we're over, and the sooner everybody realizes that, the sooner we can all get on with our lives.

CHAPTER 2
BREE

I saw the hurt on Logan's face when I mentioned I was not getting sleep, and I knew exactly what he thought I meant. But he couldn't have been more wrong. There's no way I'd let another man touch me. No one but him.

I've made mistakes. Hell, I wish I'd done things differently, but I did what had to be done.

I look at the clock on the wall, knowing that Zach, the other owner, will be in soon. If Logan and I are going to have it out, this is the time to do it.

I stand up from my desk on shaky legs. Logan is not going to make this easy, but nothing worth having comes easy.

Slowly, I walk toward the door that Logan slammed moments ago.

I raise my hand and knock softly. When there's no response, I knock again, a little harder.

"What?" Logan barks.

I tense at the briskness in his voice. I remember the days when he talked to me softly. I'd never have imagined him speaking to me this way. I open the door and walk into the room.

He pushes back from his desk as if I'm going to attack him or something. "What do you want?"

I fold my hands together in front of me. "I thought we should talk."

His jaw tightens, and he just stares at me.

I lift my chin and stare at him, determined. "Logan, I just want to say—"

He cuts me off and holds his hand up. "I don't want to hear it. I don't need your apologies. I don't need your excuses. I don't need anything from you."

"If you would just listen and let me explain—"

He laughs, but it's not his normal laugh. It's harsh and hollow. He throws a hand up in the air. "You want to explain why you were on a date with another man? Why your lips were touching someone else's?"

I knew he was mad, and I can't blame him, but I was not prepared for the hurt in his voice or the sadness in his eyes. I try again. "If you would just listen—"

"Why are you here, Bree?"

I take a step toward him. "Because I thought we should talk."

He shakes his head. "No, I mean here. In Whiskey Run, in my hometown, working for my company. Why. Are. You. Here?"

It's as if I can feel the anger vibrating off him, and I can't even be mad about it. I would be the same way if I found out he was with another woman. "Logan, I know you're not going to believe this, but I'm going to say it anyway. I love—"

He shoots to his feet before I can get the whole sentence out. "Don't you dare say you love me. Love doesn't cheat. Love doesn't let you kiss another man. Love doesn't destroy…"

He stops talking, but his chest is rising and falling rapidly. He turns away as if he can't bear the sight of me. He's staring out the blinds, but the sky is still dark, so he's looking at nothing.

When he starts talking again, he seems more in control. "Bree, whatever your reasons are, you shouldn't have come here. I can forgive a lot of things, but I can't forgive cheating. I can't forgive…" His voice breaks. "What you did to us. I want you to leave."

I hold my hands up. "If we're going to work together, we really should talk about this."

He shakes his head. "You don't get it. I want you to leave Stronghold. I want you to leave Whiskey Run."

I bite my lip and cross my arms over my chest. "I can't."

He turns to look at me, and if I saw any interest before, it's now gone, completely hidden. "Why can't you?"

I lift my chin. "Because I have nowhere to go."

"Your apartment in New York—"

I shrug. "I sold it."

"Fuck." He grunts, and then his eyes light up. "I'll

give you a severance. I'll pay you the remaining nine months in your contract, and you can leave."

He might as well have punched me in the gut. "I'm not here because I want your money, Lo."

He clenches his eyes and shakes his head as if he's in pain. "Don't call me that. You lost the right to call me that."

I nod softly as my heart breaks again, but I steel myself against that pain. "I'm not going anywhere, Logan. The contract I signed was for one year, and I have nine months left. I plan to spend that time helping you build your dream. If at the end of that time you still want me gone, I'll leave, but at least I'll know I tried." I suck in a shuddering breath. "As least I'll have tried to fix us."

He glowers at me. "There's no us. There's no we. There's nothing that can be fixed between you and me. You're wasting your time."

I nod, and before I start crying, I turn on my heel and walk out the door. Softly, I close it behind me and bypass my desk as I walk to the bathroom. *I will not cry. I will not cry*, I tell myself over and over. I clench my hands, pressing my fingernails into my palms. The pain feels good. It's weird, but in a way, it reminds me

I'm still alive. I survived the last two years, and I'll continue to do so, but I want more than just barely living. I want the life I had when I was loved by Logan.

I turn on the faucet and throw some water on my face. After drying myself off, I walk out of the bathroom and go back to my desk. I only have a few minutes to collect myself before Zach walks in. His smile disappears when he sees me. "Didn't sleep well last night either?"

I shake my head sadly.

He puts his hands on his hips. "You should really talk to someone about the nightmares."

My eyes flick to Logan's closed door. I definitely don't want him to know about my nightmares. Not like this. When and if I tell him, he needs to hear the whole story, and he's obviously not ready for that.

Ignoring his statement, I force a smile to my face. "I guess congratulations are in order."

His smile widens. "How'd you know?"

I laugh. "I'd say everyone knows. Skyler posted to her ClipClap and FriendSpace. I even saw some video from the proposal. Good job, boss man."

He laughs and claps his hands together. "Yeah, I still can't believe she said yes. I'm going to have to seal the deal before she changes her mind."

I roll my eyes. "Please. She loves you. She won't be changing her mind."

Zach crosses his arms over his chest. "So Logan is already here, I see."

I answer him with just a nod.

He leans down to look at me. "You okay?"

I lift my shoulders. "Yeah, I'm okay."

He looks at the closed the door with a frown. "Did you tell him?"

I shake my head. "Nope. He's not ready to listen."

He looks at me curiously. "What if he's never ready?"

I've wondered the same thing, but I refuse to believe it. "Eventually, he'll have to. I won't leave Whiskey Run without telling him everything."

He looks at me with pity. Ever since I told him my story, he's changed the way he's treated me. It's like he's been protective of me, and I know that fact is going to kill Logan. He wants to hate me, and he's not going to like the fact that his best friend is protective of me. He gestures to Logan's door. "If it gets too bad, tell me, and I'll take care of it."

I hold my hand up to stop him. "Zach, I can take care of myself. I'm fine."

He opens his mouth to say something but then snaps it closed. He hesitates. "I'm going to take a little time off. You can reach me, but with Logan back in town, I want to spend some time with Sky."

I nod with a smile even though I'm already dreading it. If this morning is any kind of indication of how the next nine months are going to be, it would be nice to have some kind of buffer, but I get it. Zach has been nose to the grindstone, taking care of everything these last three months, and he deserves a little time off. "Sure, I'll do my part, boss. No worries."

He nods uncertainly. "You can still call me. I'll be in and out."

I nod. "It's fine. I'll be fine."

He sighs loudly and then points to Logan's door. "Okay, well, I'm going in."

I roll my eyes. He acts like he's going in for torture

or something. "You'll be fine. It's not you he hates…"

But as soon as I start, I stop because Logan has been mad at Zach since he hired me behind his back. He was even angrier when he found out about the one-year contract I signed without an out clause. "Yeah, on second thought, good luck."

He grimaces and then walks off. He doesn't knock; he just opens the office door and walks in, closing it behind him. Instantly, voices are raised, and I decide to put my earbuds in. Regardless of everything, I have work to do, and I wasn't lying. I'm determined to help Logan get his business off the ground. Even if he doesn't want me to. He talked about his dreams, and I listened. If we can't be together, I can at least know I helped him live the life he wanted.

CHAPTER 3
LOGAN

"What do you want? I have things to do."

My best friend, the traitor, acts as if I didn't say anything and falls into the seat across from my desk, steepling his hands together at his chest. "You still hate me?"

I open my mouth to say yes, but I can't bring myself to do it. Zach and I have been through some shit together through the years, and he was always someone I could depend on. Yeah, I'm pissed at him, but I don't hate him. "I want to see this contract."

"What contract?" he asks, perplexed.

I grit my teeth, not wanting to even say her name.

"The contract you signed with Bree. I'm sure there's some kind of loophole."

He ignores me and looks around my office. "What do you think of your office? Hell, I should have had Bree decorate mine. This is nice."

I just grunt. Yeah, the office is nice, but there's no way I'm going to give her any credit for anything. "What do you want, Zach?"

He leans forward and rests his elbows on his knees. "I thought after last night, we were okay. I mean, you seemed okay last night."

I glare at him. "You were asking my baby sister to marry you. What was I supposed to do? Challenge you to a fight in the front yard? Or hell, maybe I could have punched you in that pretty boy face for the camera."

Zach nods. "I know. You're mad, and I get it. Thank you for not ruining last night. It's killing Sky that you're pissed at me. She wants us all to get along."

I move to the edge of my seat. "First, she's my baby sister, and I'd rather cut off a limb than have her upset. You can tell her that we're good, but you need to know that what you did is fucked. I mean, so fucked. If you knew… if you knew what she did, you wouldn't have hired her."

He doesn't seem surprised. Calmly, he nods his head. "I know what she did. She told me."

My mouth falls open. "And you still hired her? You hired her knowing that she…" I let my voice trail off because I can't even say the words.

Zach clears his throat. "I hired her without knowing anything. I knew you loved her, and then I knew you broke up. That's all you told me. I didn't know… until after I hired her."

I glare at him. "And what? She just give you a sob story and you forgave her?" I hold my hand up. "You know what? Forget it. I don't want to hear it. I don't even want to talk about her." I point between Zach and me. "We are not going to talk about Bree Banks any more. Not now, not ever. I'm going to look at this contract, and if there isn't a loophole, at the end of the nine months, she's gone. No ifs, ands, or buts."

He opens his mouth to say something but stops suddenly. "Fine. I did what I thought was best, and just so you know, after talking to her and hearing her side, I knew it was the right thing—"

"We're not talking about her, Zach."

He blows out a breath in frustration. "Fine. Well, I came in here to let you know that I'm taking some time off. I'm going to work from home, so you and"—he points toward the door—"she are going to hold the fort down."

I lift my chin. I want to argue, but I pretty much deserted him these last three months, and I don't blame him for taking some time off. He deserves it. "Fine. What about the party or whatever the hell you have planned?"

He laughs. "You mean the sponsorship we did for the community center? It's next Friday night, and we bought three tables."

I look at him blankly until he continues. "We're all going. That was a big job for us, and King is a good connection to have. We all need to show up."

I scowl at him. "Black tie?"

He nods and is smiling even though I know he feels the same way. He doesn't like to dress up either. "Yes, black tie. I can't wait to twirl Skyler around the dance floor."

I scrunch my nose at him. "Who the hell are you and what did you do to my best friend?"

Before he can answer, I ask him another question. "What about Bree? She going?"

Zach gives me an exasperated look. "Yes, she's part of Stronghold. She's going."

We stare at each other. There's so much I want to say to him, but I don't dare open my mouth. There's something going on here, and I don't know what it is. If Zach knows that Bree cheated on me, he wouldn't have kept her around. Hell, contract or not, he would have gotten rid of her. Something is not adding up.

Without another word, Zach gets up, but before he gets to the door, I say his name. "Zach."

He turns with a smile on his face.

"Thank you."

He raises his eyebrows in surprise. "What are you thanking me for?"

I stand up and walk around my desk. I should have done this last night, but there was so much happening that I didn't. Now I can't let another second go by without saying it. If anything, with my history in the military and working for the Ghost Team, I know you don't leave things unsaid. "Thank you for loving my sister. I know you will always protect her, and she couldn't ask for a better man than you."

He opens his mouth but then closes it as I continue. "You've always been like a brother to me. Now it's going to be official. Welcome to the family, brother."

He pulls me into a hug, and I chuckle, knowing that years of sleeping in deserts, jungles, or on the ground in makeshift beds has brought us to this moment. Zach and I have been through a lot together, and sometimes I question how we made it through some of the things we did. But here we are.

Zach tightens his arms around me as if he knows what he's about to say is going to set me off. "Listen to her, brother. Really, listen to her. You deserve happiness too."

He releases me and slaps me on the back. "I'll see you. I'm going to grab my laptop and some files. Sky and I are going to some beach for a few days, and then we'll be back."

I nod and grimace, not wanting any details of what he's going to be doing with my sister. "Have fun and take care. I'll deal with this," I tell him, waving my hand around.

He nods, opens his mouth, and then closes it. He seems to think about it and then shrugs as if he's saying fuck it. "Look, I'm not saying you have to be nice, but Bree's been beat down and well… all I'm saying is I don't know how much more she can take."

My eyebrows lift in surprise. What the hell does he mean she's been beat down? I forget my rule of not talking about her. "What do you mean—"

He cuts me off by holding his hands up. "It's not my story to tell, Logan, but maybe you should ask her."

I want to argue with him, but I simply cross my arms over my chest and nod. "Okay. See you. Call if you need anything."

He nods. "You too."

As soon as he walks out of my office and closes the door behind him, I want to jerk it open and demand answers. But instead of going off half-cocked, I stalk over to my chair and sit down. It doesn't take long before I figure it out. Whatever Bree told Zach was a lie. That's the only thing I can think of. There's no way if she told him the truth that Zach would just accept it. Yeah, that was it. She lied to him. And now Zach thinks I overreacted or something. Hell, it's impossible to guess what she told him.

I turn my chair to look out the window. The sun is up, and the streets of downtown Whiskey Run are busy with people going to Red's Diner or Sugar Glaze Bakery for their breakfast. People are off to meetings, or taking their kids to school, or whatever. As I stare at the passersby, I get lost in the memory of the third date I had with Bree.

By that point, I knew I was going to marry her. I had already told my brothers and my sister that I'd found the woman I was going to marry. I knew it was too soon, and I was biting the bullet, holding back until a decent amount of time had passed before I asked her. But by that third date, I knew.

My mission was over. I should have been back at headquarters, but I had requested some time off. Walker gave it to me. Hell, I'd never had a vacation, so I was due.

Bree was wearing a long red dress that hugged her curves in every way. I couldn't take my eyes off her. To the point where she stopped right on the middle of the sidewalk in Brooklyn. She glared up at me and crossed her arms over her chest. "All right, spill it."

She looked mad, and my smile got even bigger. "Spill what?"

She lifted a hand and touched my chest. I reached for her, holding her palm right over my heart, loving the feel of her soft skin. She rolled her eyes. "You're being quiet, and you just keep staring at me."

I licked my lips, wanting to kiss her right there on the street. When I didn't say anything, she stomped her foot, and I remember thinking how adorable she was. "Logan… what is this?" She frowned and shook her head. "I mean, if you're ending this, then just do it."

I grabbed both her hands and tugged her against my chest. "Ending this? Honey, you and me, we're just getting started."

She let out a little sigh. "Then why are you just staring at me?"

I leaned down so that our mouths were just inches apart. "You really want to know?"

She nodded, her eyes soft.

I brought a hand up and wrapped it around the side of her neck. Her pulse was racing, beating against my thumb, and I caressed her there. "I can't stop staring at you because you're beautiful. Because I can't believe you're here with me. Because I want you so much that I can barely hold back."

She let out a little whimper. "Well then, what are we doing here?"

I shook my head in confusion, and she tugged at my shirt as she looked up and down the street. "We're closer to your hotel than to my apartment. Want to go there?"

My heart literally flipped in my chest. "You want to go back to my hotel with me?"

She didn't even hesitate. "Yeah, I do. I know it's crazy. I know we just met three days ago and that we should wait, but I don't want to." Her big green eyes flickered up at me. "I want you as much as you want me, Lo."

I couldn't resist. I leaned down and pressed my lips to hers. We had kissed before but nothing like this. This kiss was everything. I put everything I was feeling, everything I was wanting into that kiss and as our lips meshed against each other, I knew that by the end of the night I was going to tell her I loved her. It might have been insane, but everything about us just felt right.

She whimpered, and I broke off the kiss. With her wide eyes looking up at me, I asked her, "You sure?"

She smiled, and it lit up her whole face. "You have to ask me after that kiss? Yeah, I'm sure."

I picked her up in my arms and swung her around, and then she pulled from my hold, grabbed my hand, and started pulling me in the direction of the hotel. That was a night I'll never forget. Never.

The ringing of my phone draws me out of my daze, and I pick it up. "This is Logan."

"Line two is for you."

Bree. I didn't even think about her being on the other end of the line, and after thinking about that first night together, my half-hard manhood goes full mast. "Thanks," I grunt before hanging up and pushing the button.

I clench my eyes shut as I listen to the caller ask about our services. I schedule a meeting for the afternoon, and all the while, I sit here not even thinking about Stronghold or the client on the phone. Nope, I'm thinking about the curvy brown-haired woman in the other room that still has a hold on my heart. It's obvious that no matter what, she's going to have a hold on me. There's no escaping it.

CHAPTER 4
BREE

I've never been more ready for a day to be over than I am now.

As I'm preparing for the two o'clock meeting, Alex and Sam walk in the door. I force a smile that I'm not feeling to my face. "Hey, guys, how'd it go?"

Alex hands me the clipboard. "Three full-service installations and one camera installation. All the paperwork is complete and filled out, and I think Sam here is ready to go on his own."

I flip through the pages on the clipboard. It's been a process. Stronghold Security has been a lot busier than Zach thought it would be, and we needed a system to streamline what we were installing, the current inventory, and an automatic ordering system. It took me a bit to get it all organized, but I think it's working well. When I see that everything is in order, I smile. "Great job, guys."

They both smile, and I look at Sam. "So you feeling good about it all? You know you can call any of us if you get in a bind or need help."

Sam blushes. He has a crush on me, but I act like I don't know about it. Both Zach and Alex have talked to me about it to make sure I wasn't uncomfortable. Sam clears his throat. "I feel like I'm ready."

I pick up another clipboard. "Great. We got a call for another installation. It's in the city limits. You wanna go?"

Sam sucks in a deep breath and lets it out. "Yes."

I hand him the clipboard. "Great, just call Alex if you have any problems."

As Sam walks out the door, Alex points a thumb over his shoulder. "Logan in his office?"

I nod, and he says, "Cool. I'm going to go check in with him." He gives me a questioning look. "You doing okay?"

I force another fake smile. "Yeah, I'm doing good."

He doesn't believe me, but he doesn't ask me any more questions as he knocks on Logan's closed door and then lets himself in.

I no sooner sit down than the front doorbell rings, and a woman walks in.

"Hello. How can I help you?"

The woman is dressed to the nines with heels and everything. She has long eyelashes, big, pouty lips, and her breasts are so high it's hard not to stare. She looks around the office. "I'm here to see Logan Brody."

I look down at the notepad. Logan came out of his office earlier and begrudgingly told me he'd scheduled an appointment for two o'clock today. That was the only time I'd seen him. "Are you Amy Burkhardt?"

She nods. "Yes, that's me."

I look at the clock. She's ten minutes early. "Have a seat. He's in a meeting right now but will be out shortly."

She takes a seat and then leans toward me and whispers loudly, "So is he still as handsome as he was in high school?"

I grit my teeth and stand, barely able to hold back an eye roll. "You want to follow me to the conference room? I'll get you set up, and I'm sure he'll be right in."

Her heels click-clack behind me as I open the door to the conference room. With a hospitality that I'm not feeling, I ask, "Can I get you something to drink? We have water, coffee, or tea."

She points to her perfectly painted lips. "Thank you, but I don't want to ruin the lipstick."

I almost crack the pen I'm holding. "Right. Well, I'll go let Logan know you're here."

I walk out of the conference room and knock on Logan's door. He must know it's me because I hear the snarly voice he seems to save for me say, "What?"

I open the door and peek in. "Your two o'clock is here. I put her in the conference room."

He nods and then waves at me as if I'm dismissed. I walk to my desk, pick up a notepad, and then head back to the conference room.

I sit down across from Amy. "Logan should be joining us soon."

She sits up a little taller and pushes her breasts out even farther. She has a smile pasted on her face as if it's frozen there.

Normally with Zach, I get the conversation going, but I'm not sure what Logan expects, and I sure as hell don't want to piss him off even more than he already is. So I sit here quietly, writing on my notepad.

I write the client's name at the top with the date and the time of the meeting. A lot of this is just habit that carried over from my last job, but I figure it doesn't hurt to be extra organized.

Only a few minutes go by before Logan walks into the room. His gaze falls on me immediately, and he frowns, but before he can say anything, Amy is bouncing from her seat. "Logan, it's so good to see you. I didn't mention this on the phone, but we went to school together. Do you remember me?"

Logan is not one to placate anyone. "I'm sorry. I don't remember an Amy Burkhardt."

She playfully slaps him on the chest and blinks her fake lashes at him. "I was Amy Ringer in high school. I was married, but now I'm single."

Her admission leaves the room in silence until Logan tries to take back control of the situation. "Well, Amy, it's good to see you again. Let's have a seat and we can talk about why you're needing our services."

She nods and throws her hands out wide. "Right, well I want the whole thing. Cameras, alarms, all of it."

My leg is going a hundred miles a minute under the table. I'm tense and ready to pull Amy's fake blond hair from her head. "How many square feet is your home, Amy?" I blurt out.

Logan tenses just hearing my voice. He holds a hand up. "I'm sorry, can you excuse us for a minute?"

Amy is taken aback but nods her head. Logan stands up and gestures to the door. "Bree, can I see you for a minute?"

I leave my notebook lying on the table and uncross my legs. "Sure."

I stand up and follow him out the door and into his office. I stop a few feet away from him and wait for him to say something.

He gestures behind me. "What was that?"

Perplexed, I wrack my brain because I have no idea what he's talking about. "What was what?"

His jaw tightens, and he cracks his knuckles. "Why were you in my meeting?"

Stunned, I rear back. "Oh. Uh, Zach always had me sit in on his meetings. It saved time because then I knew what to order, what dates and times we had available for installations, and everything."

His silence is too much for me, and I can't stand it. "I mean, if you'd rather meet with big boobs on your own, that is perfectly fine with me."

Even I can hear the jealousy in my voice, and I hate it.

Logan opens his mouth. I wait for him to tell me to go to my desk or to go to hell or something, but he actually smiles at me. "You know what? You can sit in."

He turns away, and I can only follow him back to the conference room. The rest of the meeting has me wishing that I'd never met Logan Brody. It's obvious he knew I was jealous and is really playing it up now. He's openly flirting with Amy, and it's taking everything in me to remain in my seat. By the end of the meeting, I'm staring down at the notepad and refusing to look up.

I just can't do it.

Seeing him smile at the woman across from him as they make flirty touches with each other makes me crazy.

"Bree," Logan says.

When I hear my name, I look up, and there's no hiding the hurt on my face. "Yeah?" I ask, void of any emotion.

Logan is surprised by the look on my face, and I shake my head. "Sorry. What are you asking me?"

For the first time in three months, he speaks to me softly. "When is our first available appointment?"

"Alex has availability in the afternoon next Tuesday."

Amy gasps. "Alex? But no, I don't want just anyone at my house. Can you do it?" she asks Logan.

I'm about to throw my pen at her when Logan nods. "Sure."

He looks at me. "Put her down for Friday afternoon."

I nod, jotting down the note even though I know I don't need to write it down. There's no way I won't be thinking about this stupid appointment the rest of the week.

Because I can't take another minute of this, I push away from the table and stand up. "Well, I'll let you two finish up."

Without another glance at them, I walk out of the room. It's at least fifteen minutes before they come out of the conference room, and then Logan walks Amy out to her car. My stomach revolts, and I feel like I'm going to be sick.

Seeing Logan with another woman, watching as she pawed at him and flirted, literally tore my heart to shreds. It physically hurt to watch.

That's how Logan felt.

I don't know where the thought came from, but now that I've thought it, I can't get it out of my head. I'm sure it killed him to see me at dinner with another man. I'm sure he felt sick seeing me kiss someone else when I belonged to him.

The day has caught up to me, and I can't hold it in a second longer. I shut down my computer and grab my laptop and purse. I stop by Alex's office and knock on the open door. "Hey, I need to go. Can you lock up today?"

Surprised doesn't even begin to cover it. I don't blame him. I haven't left early one day in the last three months. Hell, I've worked overtime most days, but I can't be here when Logan comes in from walking Amy to her car, probably with that bright red lipstick on his lips.

"Sure, I got it. Go."

I give Alex a nod, and then I'm walking to the back door to make sure I don't run into Logan. There's no way I'm explaining why I have to leave early. I'll just let him come to his own conclusions. I'm going home to pour myself a drink and do my best to get the image of Logan and Amy out of my head.

CHAPTER 5
LOGAN

I come in early the next day, and I'm surprised that Bree is not already at her desk.

Yesterday, she left while I was walking Amy Burkhardt to her car. Hell, that was the only way I could get her out of the office, and by the time I got back inside, Bree was gone, and Alex said she'd had to leave.

I thought about her all night.

I'm not sure why, but I felt like I owed her an apology, which is crazy. I don't owe her anything. Well, at least not for flirting with Amy. Maybe I do owe her apology for being an ass to her, though.

If my mom knew, she'd have me by the ear for treating a woman like I did yesterday.

It's exactly eight when I hear the front door open, and I don't even have to see her to know it's Bree. It's as if my body is attuned to her and knows she's close.

I'm on my feet and standing next to her desk before she can even set her things down. She doesn't look at me as she unpacks her laptop and notebooks. "Bree," I start.

She looks at me, defeated. "Yeah, Logan?"

The sadness in her voice is disarming. "You okay?"

She nods. "Yeah, do you need something?"

I clear my throat. "Yeah, can we talk?"

Her eyes light up, but I raise a hand. "I mean about work."

Her smile fades, but she picks up a notebook. "Yeah, sure. Your office or the conference room?"

"Uhm… The conference room."

I pick it because it doesn't have a couch that I've already thought about laying her down on. Although there is a huge table that I could spread her out on in the conference room. I think about that as I follow her. She's wearing a tight skirt today, and I watch her ass sway back and forth as she walks.

As soon as we're in the conference room, I have to sit down or else she's going to see the bulge in my pants. "Have a seat," I tell her, gesturing across the table. I don't need her sitting anywhere near me.

She sits down with her pen in hand as she looks down at the notebook. She's avoiding my gaze, and that should make me happy, but right now, it's irritating. "Look at me, Bree."

She raises her eyes with a stubborn look on her face and still says nothing.

I hold a hand up. "First, I want to apologize for yesterday."

She doesn't even try to hide the surprise, and for some reason, that bothers me. She has to know I'm not some kind of asshole that gets off on treating women poorly. "No matter how I feel about you or our past, I shouldn't have treated you like I did. I'm sorry."

She doesn't acknowledge my apology, so I continue. "I wanted to ask you if you'd had time to think about my offer yesterday."

Her forehead creases. "Your offer? You mean the one where you offered to buy out my contract?"

I nod. "Yeah, that's the one. Have you reconsidered?"

She sits up a little taller. "Logan, let me give you something to think about. In the three months I've been here, I've brought your company into the black."

I start to talk, but it's her turn to raise her hand. "I've hired three full-time bodyguards and have them scheduled out for the remainder of the year. And we've hired four full-time installers, and at the rate we're going right now, we need three more to keep up with the work that my advertising has brought us. It was your dream to be profitable in the first year, and I made it happen in the first three months."

I'm about to dispute her claim when she drops a bombshell. "And this is without the two hundred and fifty thousand dollars your brother Miller invested into the company."

I rear back, surprised. "What do you mean?"

She lifts her chin. "Zach didn't feel right taking that money to protect Skyler, so he hasn't touched a penny of it. It's in a separate account, earmarked for you."

She angrily leans toward me. "And so help me, Logan Brody, if you offer me that money to get rid of me, you and I are going to have problems."

Anger doesn't even begin to describe it. She's furious just thinking about it. I hold my hands up, palms out. "I wouldn't think of it."

She jerks her head up and down. "Good, but if you need ideas on how to spend that money to expand, I have them."

I know when I'm had. Zach and I had this dream and wanted to make it a reality, but our training did not equip us for this side of the business. If it was just Zach and me, we would be working out of a half-empty office with no clients and a team that didn't know what they were doing day to day. There's no doubt she's made progress here, and I guess I'd better take advantage of the situation because in nine months, she's gone. "Fine. I'd like to see the report."

She nods. "I'll email it to you when I get to my desk. Is there anything else we need to discuss?"

I open my mouth and then close it. I told myself I wasn't going to ask, but after seeing the lines around her eyes, I know I'm going to. I gesture to her face. "Why are you having trouble sleeping?"

She pinches her lips together, and I shake my head. "Don't lie to me. Just tell me. Why are you having trouble sleeping?"

She inhales and slowly blows it out. "Nightmares. I've been having nightmares."

I wasn't prepared for that answer. "What do you mean, you're having nightmares?"

She shrugs. "It's not your problem, Logan. While we're here, can I go over a few things with you?"

Dumbly, with my mouth hanging open, I nod my head. I want to go back to talking about the nightmares, but obviously, she's not having it. "Sure."

She flips through the pages of her notebook. "Sam went on his first call yesterday on his own, and he did great. Are you okay with him getting his own assignments the rest of this week?"

I tilt my head to the side. I've been gone three months. I don't even think I've met Sam yet. "What do you think?"

She rears back, blinking at me. She didn't expect me to ask that. After yesterday, I can't say I blame her. "Well, uh, I think he's ready. And if he needs anything, he can call Alex or me."

I nod. "Okay, sounds good."

She flips through more pages and stares down at some notes as she speaks to me. "There is a fundraiser next Friday night. We sponsored three tables. Should I put you down for one ticket? Or are you bringing a date?"

"Uh, put me down for two tickets." I've known about this fundraiser for a few weeks, and my brother Penn has been worried about me, so he set me up for a date with one of the nurses at his hospital.

Her face turns red, and she nods as she stands up without looking at me. "Okay, I think that's it."

She turns to go, but I stop her. "Two more things."

I can see her pull her shoulders back, sucking in a breath as if she is preparing herself for something unpleasant. I wait patiently for her to eyes to settle on me, but when she does, it's shocking. She's upset. I'm not sure what to make of this. She cheated on me. She broke us. Is she really bothered that I might take a date to a party? It's not adding up.

She puts a hand on the chair in front of her and clenches it. "Sure. What do you need?"

You. That's the first thought I have. I need her, and the fact that I feel it makes me hate myself. I grit my teeth. "First, I wanted to make sure that Guy has a ticket."

She bites her lip as she searches her memory. "Guy… your brother… the baseball player?"

I stand up and put my hands in the front pockets of my pants. "Yeah, he'll be in town, and I wanted to make sure he had a ticket for the event."

She hugs the notepad to her chest. "Yeah, Zach made sure every one of your siblings had a ticket."

I shift my stance. "Okay, lastly, I need to learn this computer program you've set up."

She looks at me blankly, so I remind her. "The one that handles the inventory, the installers' schedules, all that."

She nods, lifts her notepad, and starts writing. "Of course. I'll have a training manual for you by the end of the week."

I clear my throat and cross my arms over my chest. Bree knows me. Hell, she knows me better than anyone, and she knows that I'm not going to want a training manual. I clear my throat. "I'd rather you train me."

She points at her chest. "Me? I'm sure Alex—"

I cut her off and take a step toward her. "Alex is out of the office all day. It makes more sense for you to show me."

I'm not sure why, but I like that I still make her flustered. I'm not sure she realizes it, but she takes the notepad and uses it to fan herself. Then she realizes what she's doing and drops the papers to her side. "Yeah, sure, no problem. I'm booked up today... but this week, for sure."

I can't get another word out before she's running from the room.

I came in here today determined to keep to myself, and already I've forced a meeting with Bree and now have set up a training that is going to force us to work closely together. Maybe I'm a glutton for punishment. Maybe I'm not as over her as I thought I was. Or maybe I just like knowing that she still wants me. Whatever the case, I know that I can't go down that road again. She broke my heart once. I'm not giving her a chance to do it again.

CHAPTER 6
BREE

All I want to do is go home. Maybe because I've spent all week avoiding Logan or maybe because later this afternoon is when he's going to Amy Burkhardt's house to install her security system. I don't know which it is, but I know that I'm done.

My phone buzzes, and I practically jump from my seat as Logan's voice comes over the air. "Bree, can I see you in my office please?"

I put my head in my hands and hold in a groan. Hiding my emotions, I answer, "Sure, I'll be right there."

I've managed to stay busy and out of Logan's way most of the week, but there's no avoiding him when he beckons. As soon as I walk into the room, I stumble over my feet. Logan is seated behind his desk, but he's pulled a chair up next to him.

The truth is, I'd give anything to work by his side, snuggled up to him, but he's made it clear that he wants nothing to do with me. Heck, I'm sure he wants this training so they won't need me anymore and he can have an excuse to get rid of me.

"What's this?" I ask, gesturing to the seat next to him.

He glances down my body and back up again before clearing his throat. "Training," he grunts.

I grip the chair back in front of me just to have something to hold on to. "Uh, I thought we could start fresh with that next week."

He stands up and pulls the chair out next to him. "No, I wanna get started this morning. I have that installation this afternoon, and I'd like to get some headway on how the system and inventory works."

I've stalled all I can. I walk around the desk and sit down in the vacant chair, setting my notepad and pen on the desk top in front of me. "Okay. First, log in to the system. After you do it once, we can check the box so it automatically logs you in with facial ID or a fingerprint."

He sits down and opens the software. I tell myself to stay professional, but this is nearly impossible. He smells just like I remember: of outdoors and warmth. Like sunshine, wind, fresh cut grass, and just all him. I find myself leaning toward him as if there's a gravitational pull. It's too much for me to resist.

"This button?"

He's gesturing to the screen with his hand, and instead of looking at where he's pointing, I'm looking at his long, thick fingers and strong forearms. I shimmy in my seat as my lower belly pulls with attraction. I knew this was a bad idea. I'm going to throw myself at him, and he's going to fire me on the spot.

When I don't answer, Logan turns his head toward me at the same time I look at him. Our faces are inches apart. I lean in, wanting to kiss him just once more. Hell, I'd give anything to have his lips on mine again. He's an addiction for me, and I don't think I'll ever have my fill.

My heart starts to race, my body trembles with anticipation, and the sound of the bell at the front door has us jerking apart.

I'm panting as if I've been running instead of just sitting here.

Logan mumbles something about how he'll check to see who it is, but I remain seated, trying to catch my breath. Seconds later, Logan appears with a stack of mail. "It was the mailman. He was asking about you. Since when do they bring it inside? We have a box at the street."

It all comes out in a jumble, but I can't make sense of any of it because my eyes are glued to the bulge between his thighs. I swear his cock twitches in his dress pants as if it's trying to tease me. With my mouth hanging open, my eyes travel up his body and don't stop until they meet his. His brown eyes, usually flecked with gold, are now black orbs filled with desire, staring back at me.

I shoot to my feet. I know that look on his face, and I'm about two seconds from being bent over this desk with Logan giving me two to three orgasms while I scream his name. He tosses the mail on the desk and then stalks toward me, not stopping until his chest is pressed against mine. "It doesn't matter that I want you. It doesn't matter that I jacked off thinking about you this morning. It doesn't matter that just looking at you makes me hard. I can't do this with you, Bree. I won't."

With a hand to my chest, I can feel the wild fluttering of my heart. "I didn't ask you to," I stutter.

He puts a hand at my waist and grips me. "Really? You're not asking for it right now?" He puts his other hand on the top of his desk. "You mean if I laid you down on this desk, you wouldn't open your legs to me?"

My nipples pucker. I wish they didn't. I wish I could resist him, but I can't. Truth is, I wouldn't tell him no. Even if it meant it was one time, I would take it. Instead of answering him, I whimper.

He sucks in a breath between his teeth. "Fuck, Bree. You would, wouldn't you? You'd let me fuck you even though I hate you."

I grimace at that. Hate is such a strong word, but I get it, and I can't blame him. I lean into him as an answer.

His body tenses, and he lifts his hand from the desk. I hold my breath until I feel it land on my inner thigh, and then I can't control the trembling. His fingers are rough, the kind that belong to a man that works outdoors, not in an office. I want to ask him if he's enjoying his retirement from the military and the Ghost Team, but I can't seem to form a thought as his hand slides up and he palms my panty-clad pussy.

His finger presses against the sodden material, and I lift my hips, wanting more.

His voice is gruff right next to my ear. "You're soaked."

He says it accusingly, as if he didn't expect it. He has to know that I'm always wet for him. I slide my skirt up higher, opening my legs. I'm practically begging for it, and when his finger skims along the edge of my panties and then slips underneath, I'm holding my breath. As soon as the pad of his finger touches my bare skin, it's like a jolt to my system. I grab his arm and hold it, my fingers digging into his flesh.

He presses his digit into my hot, wet flesh and strokes me. One pass over my clit, and I feel as if I'm going to explode. He pulls his hand from between my thighs and brings it to his lips. I watch through hooded eyes as he sucks his finger into his mouth.

He groans as his eyes devour me.

All I can do is stare at him, hungry, wanting more.

He pulls his finger from his mouth. "Fuck, you taste good."

My chest shudders, and I'm about to sit on his desk and open my legs. Hell, I'm not above begging at this point because I'm so overcome with need right now I can't stand it.

He brings his hand to my neck, and I'm expecting him to kiss me, but he stops short. His voice is angry now. "I can't forget that another man has tasted you… has kissed you… has fucked you."

He lets go of me and turns away. He puts his hands in his pockets, barely opens the blinds, and stares out the window into downtown.

I lift my hand to his shoulder, but he tenses, so I pull back. I adjust my skirt and then hug myself. "Logan, there hasn't been anyone else. No one but you."

He turns on me in an instant. "Don't lie to me, Bree. I saw you."

I try to explain. "It was a kiss… but I didn't… we didn't…"

He holds his hand up. "Stop. I don't want to hear it." He picks up my notepad and hands it to me.

"We'll save the training for another day. On second thought, I'll have Alex do it."

"But—" I start.

He lifts his chin, and I'm surprised to see absolutely no emotion on his face. "That will be all, Bree. I got what I needed from you. You can go."

I stumble backwards, pulling my skirt down as I go. Without another glance at him, I walk out of his office, drop the notepad on my desk, and then go to the restroom.

After locking the door, I lean against the counter and stare at my reflection in the mirror over the sink. Anger, regret, sadness, exhaustion… I'm feeling all of it. I'm not sure why I'm doing this to myself. But just as soon as the thought comes, I know the answer.

I stare into my own eyes, remembering the last two years without Logan. They were hell. It was the worst time of my life. I take a deep breath and know that eventually I'm going to have to answer the hard question. Is it better to be apart with him hating me or to work next to each other and feel his hate on a whole other level? Even though I'd give anything to have what we once had, I don't think I can take much more of this.

CHAPTER 7
LOGAN

At one o'clock, I know I can't avoid it any longer. I'm going to have to leave my office.

First, I change into jeans and a T-shirt, and once that's done, I walk out into the lobby. Without looking at Bree, I ask, "Is Alex in?"

"No, he's out for the afternoon with installations."

"Sam?"

"No, same."

I let my head fall back and am barely able to hold back my frustration. "Anybody else that works here?"

Her voice softens. "Nope. Just me and you."

"Fuck," I groan.

She stands up, and I can't avoid it any longer. I look at her, and as soon as I do, I know I shouldn't have. I swear I can still taste her on my tongue. Her sweet scent has stayed with me all morning, and I've sat in my office with a hard-on, thinking of all the ways I wanted to have her.

She crosses her arms over her chest. "If you tell me what you need, I can help you."

It's on the tip of my tongue to tell her that I need to get off, that these fuckin' blue balls are killing me, but I know that's a bad idea. "Grab your stuff. You're going with me."

Her eyes widen, and she freezes. "Where are we going exactly?"

I put my hands on my hips. "To the Burkhardts'."

Her face turns red, and her cheeks puff out. "I'm not going."

I take a step toward her. "Yes, you are."

She waves her hand toward my office. "Look, I get it. You want to punish me. Fine. I can take it, but I draw the line there, and I think I've had enough today."

Clueless, I shake my head, wracking my brain. "What the hell does that have to do with the Burkhardts?"

She puts a hand on her shapely hip and glares at me. "You think I want to go to watch you flirt with that woman? Newsflash. I don't."

Floored, I rear back. "Flirt with her? It's a job. You were there. We're installing a security system."

She laughs, and it sounds manic. "Oh yeah? I'm not installing anything because I'm not going."

I suck in a breath and spit out the words without thinking. "I swear I want to bend you over my knee and spank that fat ass."

She hisses a breath and glares at me through the slits of her eyes. "Oh no you didn't. You did not just say I have a fat ass."

She's pissed, and I can't lie. I love it when she gets riled up. I wish I didn't, but I do. I put my hands in the air. "Stop it. I didn't—"

She starts slamming notebooks, drawers, pens…. Hell, everything she can get her hands on. I stalk over to her and don't stop until we're chest to chest. "Are you really offended, Bree? I've licked, kissed, eaten, and fucked that ass. You know I love it, so I didn't mean anything by that comment."

I see her pulse jumping in her neck. No doubt she's remembering all the times I've spent loving on her butt, and if I don't step away, I'm going to show her right now just how much I've missed it.

I take a step back. "Grab your purse. You're going with me." I hold my hand up. "And I think you know me. Hell, you know me better than anyone. Amy is not my type."

I walk out to the van and open the passenger side door. Bree locks the front door of the office, breezes by me, and settles in the passenger seat. I resist reaching for the seat belt and putting it on her. Hell, the way she sits there, she's waiting for me to do it, but I just stand here, looking at her blankly, until she puts it on herself.

I'm about to close the door when she stops me. "I need to make a stop first."

I grit my teeth. "Why?"

She turns her head and looks me dead in the eye. "I'm not wearing any underwear. I had to remove them because they were… wet." She gestures to herself. "And I can't be climbing ladders or crawling under things in this."

I grip the door so hard my knuckles turn white. "You're not wearing any panties?"

She glares at me. "No."

I stand back and shut the door. My cock twitches between my thighs, and it's almost painful to walk around to the driver's side of the van. All I need is the image of Bree with no panties sitting at her desk. There's no way I'm going to resist this temptation for the next nine months. It's not possible.

I get in and start the van. "Where do you live?"

She lifts her chin. "Above Savage Ink."

My head turns so fast I'm surprised I don't get whiplash. "Excuse me? You live above the tattoo place?"

She nods and looks out the window, avoiding my gaze. I drive down the street, turn off Main Street, and stop at Savage Ink. Bree is out of the van before I even get fully stopped. I jump out and am one step behind her as she gets to the door.

"What are you doing?" she asks, staring at me.

I open the door and gesture for her to go in. "I'm going with you."

She doesn't budge. "Why?"

I shrug. Hell, I don't know why. I should stay in the van and mind my own business, but there's something inside me that wants to see where she is living.

When I don't answer, she stomps past me, walks up the stairs, and unlocks the apartment door. I go in behind her, leaving the door open as I walk into the open concept living room kitchen area.

She mumbles, "I'll be right back" and leaves me standing there.

I look around the bare room, disappointed that it's so empty. This is nothing like the place Bree lived in in New York. It was decorated with personal items and pictures everywhere. It screamed Bree. This doesn't.

I'm looking around, trying to sort things out in my head when someone calls from the doorway, "Who the hell are you?"

I pull my shoulders back and stare at the man covered in tattoos. "Who the hell are you?"

He walks into the apartment, holding some kind of Tupperware dish. "I asked you first. Where's Bree?"

As soon as he says her name, I practically ignite. I step toward him, toe to toe. "What business is it of yours?"

We're glaring at one another when Bree comes into the room, hopping on one foot, trying to put her shoe on as she balances on her other leg. "Logan, stop. Logan, this is Aiden. He owns Savage Ink. He's my landlord."

She gestures to me. "Aiden, this is Logan… my boss."

Aiden's face breaks out into a smile. "Oh, shit. I should have recognized you as one of the Brody brothers. Nice to meet you."

He holds his hand out to me, and I shake it grudgingly. "You always just walk into Bree's apartment when you want to?"

He smirks, not the least bit offended. Instead of answering me, he turns to Bree. "Sorry, but the door was open, and when I saw Logan standing here, I was worried it was one of the guys from the city."

"What guys from the city?" I blurt out.

Aiden looks at me round-eyed and then turns back to Bree. They both stand there mutely, not answering my question, so I repeat it. "What guys from the city?"

Bree finishes tying her shoe and stands up. She's wearing black leggings and a long green shirt with the Stronghold Security logo on the chest, and her hair is in a ponytail on the top of her head. "No one." She looks at Aiden and points at the Tupperware. "Is that for me? Gracie said you were going to drop off something."

He nods proudly. "Yep, she made some cookies to help you sleep."

Bree avoids looking at me. "Your wife is the sweetest. I'll call her later to thank her. And thank you for dropping them off."

He nods and looks between Bree and me again. "Gracie told me to tell you that if it will help, you can stay with us."

I grunt, and there's no hiding my obvious disagreement with that. "Bree, we should go."

She nods. "Right. Thank you, Aiden, truly. But the apartment is perfect, and I appreciate you and Gracie so much. Please tell her I'll call her later."

He nods, and after a few more niceties, he leaves. I'm openly staring at Bree as she walks to the still open door. "You ready?"

I follow her out, and it's not until we're in the van and halfway across town that I break the silence. "What was that about?"

She's looking out the window. "What?"

I groan, gripping the steering wheel tighter. "The cookies, the offer to stay at his house, the guys from the city. All of it, Bree. What was that?"

CHAPTER 8
BREE

It would be so easy to just spill all my secrets. I would love to be able to tell Logan everything, but there's a fear that he's going to hate me even more than he already does. I lied to him. He could easily say our whole time together was a lie, and he wouldn't be wrong. So instead of answering him, I grab a notepad from my purse. "Okay, so we should probably have a game plan going into this, don't you think?"

He squeezes the steering wheel, and when we get to a stop sign, he glares over at me. He doesn't like to be told no, and he doesn't like to be out of the loop. He's a man that just gets in there and takes care of things. Unfortunately, this is not something he can fix.

I fill the silence with my ramblings. "I'm sure Amy is going to want your undivided attention. I'm just going to work on installing the cameras. There's one at the gate, front door, and back door, and she wants one that goes into the backyard." I turn to look into the back of the van. "We have the ladders, so as long as there is a tree or a post or something, we can make it happen."

We pull onto Amy's road, and he stops before he gets to her gate. "First of all, you're not going to be climbing anything. Second, you're not leaving my side. I didn't bring you here to do the job. I brought you so that you can deal with Amy while I install. And third, you have secrets. Big ones, it seems. If you brought danger to—"

I cut him off. "I didn't. No one knows I'm here."

He watches me closely. "And these guys from the city?"

I hold my breath. "It's from my nightmares, Lo. That's all. Trust me, I wouldn't put you, your family, or your business in danger. No one can find me."

Fuck, at least I hope not.

Logan's eyebrows lift to his hairline. "What are you not telling me, Bree?"

Luckily, Amy is walking down her driveway to meet us, and I'm saved from answering. I open the door, ready to escape. "There's Amy. We'd better get to work."

I move to the back of the van and am gathering some supplies as Logan joins me. His voice is gruff next to my ear. "We're not done with this conversation, Bree."

I ignore him and turn to Amy. "Hey, Amy."

She frowns at me, and then when Logan turns toward her, her face lights up, and her voice is all husky and sex-laden. "Hey Logan."

I'm unable to hold back my groan of disgust, but I try to cover it up with a cough. I'm about to put the heavy tote over my shoulder when Logan takes it from my hand and puts it over his instead. He's looking at me but talks to Amy. "Hey, Amy, you wanna show us around?"

Amy's caught off guard but pulls herself together quickly. She leads us through the house and out the back door, showing us where she would like to have the cameras.

Every attempt to flirt with Logan or even try to get him alone fails. He's professional but curt, and it takes a while, but eventually Amy catches on that nothing is going to happen. At least not today.

It takes hours to install all the cameras, but I finally convinced Logan that I would be of better use to actually help with the install instead of just standing around, so that shortened the time some.

By the end of the appointment, I'm covered in dust, grass, and sweat, and I'm exhausted.

Amy is walking us to the van, and she sticks right with Logan, even when he opens the door for me. He almost puts my seat belt on and then catches himself and hastily shuts the door. I can't hear what he and Amy are saying as they walk around to the other side of the van, but Amy sure is smiling as she waves goodbye.

I try not to let it affect me, but I'm not good at hiding my feelings. "You know what? If the security business doesn't work out, you could probably succeed with a dating business. You can just pimp yourself out and make a fortune."

I force a laugh at the end, but Logan doesn't join in. His voice is deadpan and void of emotion. "I'll just stick to the security business."

We're quiet as we get into town until Logan breaks the silence. "Have you heard from Scott and Jo? How are their assignments going?"

Scott and Jo are two men Zach hired while Logan was out of town. They are both on bodyguard details. "Yeah, I got an email from each of them with their updates. I think Jo will be back next week. Scott will be another few weeks, but we knew his would be an extended situation. Both are good and on track."

He puts his elbow on the door. "Good. It's weird having employees and not knowing who they are."

I match his position and put my arm up in the window, but I lean out a little to let the wind hit me. "Yeah, that happens when you take off for three months."

He rolls his eyes. "I had my reasons."

He might as well say it. We're both thinking it. It's me. I'm the reason that he left his town, his family, and his new business. I'm not sure what I was thinking when I came here. Did I really believe that we could get back what we once had? I guess I had hoped, but the longer I'm here, the madder Logan gets. At what point do I call it? I have months left on my contract, but at this rate, my nerves will be shot by then. We can't just work side by side with women openly flirting with him and me unable to do anything about it.

I look over at him, and when he notices me watching him, his jaw starts to tick. I want to suggest we get dinner, but I don't bother. The answer will be no.

"What?" he asks gruffly.

I clench my hands together in my lap. "You hate me, don't you?"

He doesn't seem surprised by the question, and he doesn't attempt to answer me. The rest of the way into town, I'm staring out the window, trying to hold back tears. *I will not cry, I will not cry*, I repeat to myself over and over.

Instead of going back to the office, he parks on the side of the road, right in front of Savage Ink. I open my door, ready to get out, when he stops me by wrapping his hand around my forearm.

I stop. Heck, I stop moving, breathing, everything and just stare at him.

He shakes his head. "I want to hate you. I really do. But I can't… But none of that matters, Bree. When your contract is up, you're leaving. I won't ask you to stay."

His words gut me. I guess I should have known that would be the case. What we had was amazing and life-changing, but I messed it up. I'm the one to blame.

I tug on my arm, but he doesn't let me go. "I got it, Logan. I understand. I'm going to work for the next nine months without any expectations. I know you want me gone, but if it's okay with you, I'd like to work out my contract and figure out my next steps."

His jaw tenses, and he lets me go. "You have a contract. I don't have a say."

Basically, he wants me to know that if it was up to him, I'd be gone already.

"Right, I know, I cornered you into this. I thought…"

A dark laugh escapes him. "You thought what? You'd come here and I wouldn't be able to keep my hands off you and we'd go back to the way we were? You cheated on me, Bree. You kissed another man, you—"

"If you'd let me explain—"

He's not having it, though. He sits in his seat, stiff as a statue and grips the steering wheel. "There's nothing you can say to me that would make your actions okay." He looks over at me, and all I see is the hatred in his eyes. "Thanks for going on the call with me." Before I can answer, he smiles at me. "Amy and I are getting coffee this weekend."

I suck in a breath, and it feels like he's physically punched me in the gut. It's been two years. I figured he had been dating anyway, but seeing it and knowing it is another thing. Unable to hide the hurt, I need to escape. I jump out of the car, shut the door, and without another glance at Logan, I practically sprint to the stairs that lead to my apartment.

The hurt is unbearable, and I'm left with a feeling of complete and utter defeat. It's devastating because any hope I'd had for me and Logan is gone. I'm not sure what else I can do. He doesn't want to talk about our past or what happened. He doesn't want to hear me out. It's over... and I'm not sure what to do with that.

CHAPTER 9
LOGAN

It's been hours since I dropped Bree off, and I can't stop thinking about her. I'm nursing the same beer I got out of the refrigerator two hours ago, my feet are propped up on the coffee table, and there's something on the television, but for the life of me, I couldn't tell you what is happening on the screen.

No matter how hard I try to clear my head, all I can think about is Bree and all the unanswered questions I have.

What is it about these nightmares she's having? She never had nightmares when we were together. And what was Aiden talking about when he said he thought I could be one of the guys from the city? And then her acting like she didn't cheat on me and break my heart. Fuck, why did she look so devastated when I said I was going for coffee with Amy? She was broken-hearted, and no matter how much I want to hate her, I can't. I hated seeing that look in her eyes, but it's even worse knowing I put it there.

I lift my arm and look at my watch. Eleven o'clock.

I'm sure she's asleep. The need to talk to her or to at least know she's okay is overwhelming. I wish I could turn this need for her off, but I can't.

Without second-guessing myself, I grab my truck keys off the coffee table and stand up. I'm in shorts and a T-shirt that I changed into after my shower. I hastily put on socks and shoes and am out the door not a minute later. I'm not sure what the urgency is all about, but I just need to get to her.

I park on the side of the street and look up at her apartment window. Savage Ink is still lit up, and I can see two people in there, but Bree's light upstairs is off. I turn off my truck and just stare into her dark window. I don't know what I thought I'd see, but there's a calm that comes over me, knowing she's safe and in her bed.

The light comes on as I'm about to push the button to start my truck. My heart starts to race. Did she have a nightmare? Or is it something else?

I watch her pass by the window, and I know I can't sit out here a second longer. I grab my keys, get out, and am crossing the street with my eyes trained on her window. I try the door at the bottom of the stairs, expecting it to be locked, but it's not. I'll be addressing that with her landlord, Aiden, in the morning.

I take the stairs two at a time and don't stop until I'm standing in front of her door. I lift my hand to knock but think twice about it. It's going to freak her out if she hears someone knocking at her door this late at night. I pull my phone from my pocket and find her name in my contacts. The first thing I do is unblock her. Then I hit the button to call her.

I can hear the phone ringing in her apartment, and almost immediately, she answers. "Logan… is that you?"

"I'm standing outside your door. Come open it?"

"What… what are you doing here?"

She opens the door, and I turn the phone off and pocket it. The sight before me tells me I made the right call. Her eyes are swollen, telling me she's been crying. Her hair is wild on her head, and she looks exhausted.

I push my way into her apartment, and without saying a word, I shut the door, lock it, and kick off my shoes. I walk through the living room, down the hall, and stop outside her bedroom door. Her scent envelops me, and it's going to take all the strength I have to do what I'm thinking about doing. I turn and see that she's following behind me, watching me curiously.

"What are you doing here, Logan?"

Without answering her, I take a deep breath and walk to the side of the bed. The one she doesn't sleep on. I pull my shirt off and toss it to the chair. I ignore Bree's gasp as I pull my phone out and set it on the nightstand and then climb into bed, making sure to stay on top of the covers. I pat the bed beside me. "Come on. Lie down."

She's frozen in the doorway. "Logan… I don't think this is going to fix anything."

I grimace. She thinks I'm here to fuck her. I mean, I want to. Hell, I want to so badly my cock twitches just thinking about it, but that's not why I'm here.

I grunt in frustration. "I'm not here to fuck, Bree. I'm here so you can actually get some sleep."

She takes a step toward me and stops. "What? You're here because… I've been having nightmares?"

I shrug. "You want to sleep, right? I'm here so you can sleep."

"But—" she starts, but I don't let her finish. I know she probably has a hundred questions about why I'm here, or why I care, but I'm not ready to answer any of them.

"Get in the bed, Bree."

She just stands there, staring at me, and I sit up. "Honey, you're exhausted. I just want to give you one night of peace, that's all. This has nothing to do with your job, with our past, nothing. I just… I just need you to get some rest, okay?"

Slowly, she reaches for the light and turns off the switch. She starts walking toward the bed, and I hold my breath. She sits down next to me, sliding under the covers, and it's like she's been holding her breath too because it comes out in a whoosh.

Lying here in darkness, with only the street lamp outside coming through the blind, I can make out her eyes. She's staring at the ceiling, and I know she doesn't know what to think of all this.

"Why have you been crying, Bree?"

She clenches her eyes shut but doesn't say a word.

I turn toward her, making sure I don't touch her. Her scent surrounds me, and I want to inhale it deep into my lungs, but I don't because I know it's just torture. "Bree, talk to me."

She looks over at me. "I was upset earlier, but I shouldn't put any of it on you. It's not your job to deal with my uh, stuff."

Her answer only confuses me more, but before I can ask her to explain it, she continues. "I was crying because it hit me… we're over… and I can't do anything about it."

I want to lash out at her, but I bite my tongue. I want to ask her why she did it, why she cheated on me, but I don't. There's no reason to rehash the past because no matter what, I'll never trust her again. Not like I did.

"Talk to me about the nightmares."

"What do you want to know, Logan? They started two years ago, but they are worse lately. No matter how hard I try, I just can't sleep more than an hour or two at a time."

I put a finger to my chest. "Are you saying it's because of me and what happened between us two years ago?"

She shakes her head. "No, but after you left, I had some, uh, issues. It's been since then."

I want to ask her about it, but I don't.

"Okay, what can I do to help?"

She takes a deep breath and lets it out slowly. "I just need to feel safe, that's all."

"Safe? Are you not safe here?"

She shrugs and rolls to her back to stare up at the ceiling again. "Just forget it, Logan."

I stare at her in the darkness, and a need like I've never felt before comes over me. More than anything in this moment, I want her to feel safe. I can do that for her. Even if it's just for tonight.

My voice husky, I tell her, "Come over here."

She gasps. "What did you say?"

I groan. "You know what I said. You want to sleep, come over here and let me hold you so you can sleep."

She looks at me. "You want to hold me?"

Fuck, I wish I could say no. I shouldn't want to hold her. Hell, I shouldn't even want to be near her, but knowing she was here, hurting, scared, or whatever she's feeling was driving me nuts, and I couldn't just sit at my house and do nothing. "I want to help you sleep, that's all. You work for me, and you're no use if you're exhausted all the time."

She gasps, offended. "I'm on time every day. I work overtime most days. I'm heading off problems before they happen and—"

I cut her off. "I get it. I know. You work hard, and you've taken my dreams for my business and helped make it a reality. I owe you. So come here and let me hold you so you can try and sleep through the night."

CHAPTER 10
BREE

I shouldn't do it. I shouldn't have even let him in the house, but I can't resist him. Heck, if he wanted me, I would give in to him in an instant. But he doesn't want me. He's just here out of guilt—and the fact that he's a good and decent guy probably has something to do with it too. But if I let him hold me, I just know I'm going to be hurt… again. And hell, it's been two years, and I'm still trying to put my heart back together again.

"This is a bad idea, Logan."

He sighs. "I don't have any ulterior motive here, Bree. I know you're tired, you're scared… and if you won't tell me why, this is the only way I know I can help."

I'm staring at his bare chest, remembering what it was like to touch him and feel his warmth. He's right here, waiting for me to make the move, and I'm not strong enough to resist what he's offering. Slowly I slide across the bed, and almost shyly, I lean into him.

On contact, he sucks in a breath and tenses. I freeze with my cheek pressed against his chest. It's awkward with my body half against him, and I'm not sure what to do from here.

"Oh fuck," he groans. He fixes the covers and moves underneath them, and then he hauls me toward him, wrapping his arms around me, threading our legs together like he used to, and I can't help it. I melt into him, reveling in the feel of his arms around me. My mind quickly goes back to the past, lying in bed in my apartment in New York City with Logan by my side. He held me like this every night we were together, and I remember thinking that I never wanted him to let me go.

His voice is hard. "Are you okay?"

I nod against his chest, unable to form the words for what I'm feeling, not that he'd want to know anyway. If I thought he would listen, I would tell him everything, but fear stops me. I don't want him to get mad and walk away. I need this night in his arms. I have been numb for so long, I just need to feel something right now.

"Bree, if this bothers you, I can leave."

My arms tighten around him. "No, don't go. Please don't leave."

I am not one to beg, but I would go down on my knees right now and plead with him to stay. If I can only have this one night, I'll take it. There are so many things going through my head, and even though I know this is a bad idea, I'm not going to turn him away. "I know I don't deserve this, Logan, but I don't want you to leave."

His tense body softens into the mattress, and he holds me to him. I can feel and hear everything. His soft sigh, the thud of his heartbeat under my cheek, the warmth of his body, the way his fingers caress my back through my shirt. They're all tiny reminders of what I had and what is no longer mine.

His chin caresses the top of my head. "You going to be able to sleep?"

"Honestly?" I ask.

He nods. "Yeah, honestly. That's all I want from you, Bree. No more lies."

I clench my eyes together. He's right. I lied to him two years ago. There's so much he doesn't know about me, and I'm afraid even if I told him all of it, he wouldn't care. He'd still want nothing to do with me. So I go with the here and now. "I want to sleep. I really do. I want to be able to just close my eyes and go off to la la land, but another part of me doesn't want to." I suck in a breath and then blurt out everything I'm feeling right now. "I don't want to miss lying in your arms or feeling your body against mine. I don't want to miss that soft cooing noise you make right before you drift off to sleep. I don't want to miss any of it, Logan… because I know that this is it. Tomorrow, we'll both act like you weren't in my bed, that we didn't sleep in each other's arms. I just… I don't want to miss it. Ya know?"

He sighs softly and hugs me to him. "I know, Bree." He's silent for a few seconds, and then his deep voice fills the room. "I wish things were different for us, but there's no going back. The only thing we can hope for is some kind of friendship, honey. That's all I can offer you because you broke me.

Fuck, you broke me so badly that I'll never be the same, and I can't do that to myself again. I won't."

My heart hurts. This is pure fuckin' torture, but I don't care. Instead of pulling away or guarding my heart like I know I should, I lean into him even more. I commit it all to memory. Every feeling, every thought, every way he makes me feel because if this is the last time he holds me, I'm not going to waste it. I'm going to relish it. I put my hand to his chest and start to ramble. My fingers trace across his skin, and little goosebumps pop up. "I know you don't want to hear it. There's things you don't know about me, and it's not an excuse, but if you knew them, it might make my betrayal easier to understand."

His voice is grave. "You kissed another man, Bree, and for the rest of my life I'll have that image in my head." He sucks in a deep breath and slowly blows it out. "Go to sleep, okay?"

I close my eyes and think back to our past. We were so good together. From the instant I saw him in that bodega, I felt a special bond with him. We dated for months. He was on a mission there, and we were lucky because we were able to spend so much time together. We knew it would end, but when his mission was over, he didn't leave. He stayed in town, and we continued to date. At that time, I couldn't leave the city, but I knew eventually, when I was able, I would follow him wherever he wanted to go.

I yawn and feel myself falling into slumber. I fight it hard, but so many sleepless nights are catching up with me, and when I finally do go to sleep, tucked into Logan's arms, I'm ready for it.

I don't wake until the sun has come up, and I'm in my bed alone. I stretch my arms and legs out, then look at the pillow next to my head. There's an indentation, but any hopes that Logan is still here are slowly dashed. He's gone. I don't even have to lift my head to look or call out his name. I know he's gone.

I lie back on the pillow and think about the night before. He didn't have to come, and he didn't have to stay, but he did. He mentioned us being friends, and I grimace replaying his words in my head. I don't want to be friends with him. I want so much more.

I lift up to my elbows and can't help but smile. I slept through the night. I didn't have one nightmare, and I know I have Logan to thank for that.

I reach for my phone that is plugged in on the nightstand. I unplug it and look at the time and then shoot up in bed. Nine o'clock! I slept until nine o'clock. My alarm didn't even go off.

I jump out of bed and run to the bathroom. I'm glad I showered last night because I'm going to have to rush to get to work. I dial Logan's number frantically. "Logan!"

He's on high alert. "What is it? What's wrong?"

"I overslept. I'm so sorry. I'll be there as soon as I can. The alarm didn't go off and—"

He cuts me off. "Bree, stop. It's Saturday. There's no work today. I turned off your alarm because I knew you had probably set it and I wanted you to get as much sleep as you could. I left you a note."

I gasp and walk back into the bedroom, looking for a note. I grip the phone tighter as I walk into the kitchen and spot it on the counter. "You turned off my alarm?"

His voice is husky. "Yeah, you were sleeping so good, I wanted to let you rest."

I scan the note he left me. *Hey Bree. I know you're going to be in a full blown panic this morning when you find out I turned off your alarm. Take the day off. I know you've been working weekends and you should take the weekend off. Logan*

"Bree, you there?"

I hold the note in my hand. He wrote it on a Post-it note that he must have gotten from my desk. "Yeah, I'm here. Thank you again. For last night, I mean."

I hang up before I do something stupid like tell him I still love him. I toss my phone onto the counter and lean my head back with my eyes clenched closed. Last night was the best night of sleep I've had in a long time. It's hard to tell how tonight is going to go, but at least I got one good night's rest. I'm not sure what I'm going to do today if I'm not going to the office, but I know I need to get ready for Monday when I face the man whose heart I broke and who I would give anything to have love me again.

CHAPTER 11
LOGAN

Walking out of Bree's apartment was hard this morning. But getting out of her bed was damn near impossible. I wanted to roll her to her back and slide into her, but I resisted. She slept through the night. That was what I wanted, and it happened, but now I can't stop thinking about her. I went to the gym and ran harder than I had in a long time, just trying to expend some of this extra energy.

I went to my sister's house, and she made me try a bunch of new recipes she's been experimenting with. I caught Zach up with what's been happening in the office, and then I checked in with each of my brothers and reminded them all about the fundraiser next week. I went back to Savage Ink and had a talk with Aiden. After getting his approval, I redid the security system for the door that leads to the apartment upstairs, and after leaving the instructions with Aiden, I hightailed it out of there. I was hoping to avoid seeing Bree, but in a way I was secretly hoping to see her too, so I'm not sure what I'm doing with myself these days.

At eleven o'clock at night, I find myself sitting in my truck outside of Bree's apartment again. I'm a fool, that's what I keep telling myself. I know this is a bad idea, and I know I should stay away from her, but I can't help it. There's something deep inside me that needs to know she's okay.

For an hour, I sit here watching her bedroom window, and when I see the light come on, I know she's having trouble sleeping.

I do the same as I did the night before, except this time, I use a code to get inside the door downstairs. When I'm stationed outside her door, I call her.

It rings five times, and instead of answering, she's opening the door with a big smile on her face. She leans against it. "Is this how it works? I turn my bedroom light on and you magically appear?"

I kick off my shoes next to the door and stroll past her silently.

"Aiden wouldn't tell me who put the security system on the door downstairs, but I know it was you."

I just grunt as I walk into the bedroom and take my shirt off, tossing it to the chair in the corner. I sit down on the edge of the bed and watch her as she leans against the door. I pat the bed beside me. "Well, come on. You're not going to sleep standing there."

She walks toward the bed and sits down next to me. "What are we doing here, Logan?"

I jut my chin at her. "You can't sleep. I'm staying so you can sleep."

She leans toward me, pink-cheeked, and her voice is barely a whisper. "What if I don't want to sleep?"

I sit up straighter. I thought I could come in here, hold her for the night, and then leave before she gets up in the morning. I keep saying I'm doing this for her, but I'm doing it for me too. I want to hold her. Fuck, I need it.

"Bree…" I start.

She shakes her head. "Forget it. You're right. I appreciate you doing this."

She lies down and pulls the covers up over her body. I blow out a slow breath. This is too much temptation, and I'm not sure how long I can resist her, but I'm willing to try. "You coming over here?"

She slides toward me and presses her curvy body into my side. I wrap my arms around her, and she snuggles closer. A few seconds go by, and she squirms as if she's having trouble getting comfortable.

"You okay?"

She nods against my chest.

Without thinking about it, I stroke my hand up and down her back soothingly.

Eventually we're going to have to talk about us, but I don't want to do it now. This is too intimate, and when we do talk, I need to have a clear head.

Bree's breathing starts to even out, and she softens into me. I know the instant she's asleep because her little sighs stop.

I should sleep, but I don't. My body is wired and hard, and I steel myself against the temptation of having her in my arms.

She pulls her leg up across my body, and it touches my hard manhood. The groan leaves me before I can stop it. She jerks awake, lifting her head and looking at me in surprise. She doesn't move her leg. If anything, she presses her thigh more firmly against my erection, and I groan again. Without thinking, I put a hand on her ass to hold her still. "Fuck, Bree, don't move."

Her voice is low and husky. "Logan…"

It's like I can hear the need in her voice. I should put some distance between us, but instead I grip her ass in my hands, holding her to me.

She puts a hand on my chest and leans up to look at my face. "Logan, please… I know how you feel about me, but—"

She stops, and I ask, "But what?"

She blinks at me. "But it's like I'm numb. For the past two years, it's like I can't feel anything. I want to feel again…"

She's tracing her finger against my chest, and I suck in a breath as she drags her hand downward and then cups me through my thin shorts. My hips surge forward, and instinctively, I push Bree to her back and hover over top of her. I grind my pelvis against hers, and with a moan, my mouth almost touching hers, I warn her, "This doesn't mean anything… we're just blowing off steam… that's all this can be."

I see the hurt flash in her eyes, but then she nods. As soon as she agrees, I can no longer hold back. I lean in, and as soon as our lips touch, I'm a goner. The chemistry between us is undeniable. It's a mashing of teeth, tongues sliding along each other, moans, and pure longing.

I pull back and search her eyes. "Are you sure?"

She loops her hand around my neck and pulls me back down to her. Her kiss is my answer. I cup her breast, but the material is in my way. I want to feel her soft body against mine. Quickly, I remove her shirt, shorts, and panties. She stretches out, arching her back, and I cup her full breasts in my hands. I pluck her nipples between my thumb and forefinger, and she gasps, pushing into it.

I suck her nipple into my mouth, swirling my tongue around her. I move to the other one, and her hand slides down my body, cupping me through my shorts.

"You're wearing too many clothes," she moans.

I pop off her breast and pull down my shorts and underwear and then hover over her. She circles her hand around my girth, squeezing me, and I groan. Fuck, she feels good.

"What do you need?" I ask her.

She moans. "You… inside me. I don't want to wait."

I stare into her eyes. "There hasn't been anyone since you… I'm safe."

She nods, never looking away, and repeats what I just said. "There hasn't been anyone since you."

A part of me wants to scream because I still think about the man she kissed, but I know Bree, and she wouldn't lie about something like this.

She opens her thighs and guides me to her entrance. "Please, Logan."

Slowly, I slide into her. She's snug and tight, wrapped around me, and I still, inhale deeply, and then enter her completely. I feel as if I have to pause and catch my breath. This still feels good. It feels perfect… like I'm home.

"Fuck, you feel good," I moan.

Her hands go up my body to my shoulders. She bites her bottom lip and tightens around me, hooking her legs around my hips, pulling me deeper. I'm fighting the need for release, wanting this to last, afraid of what will happen afterward.

I take it all in. How her chest rises and falls with every hitched breath, the soft whimpers she makes, the way she's looking at me under hooded eyes as if I hung the fuckin' moon.

"Please… don't stop," she begs.

I slowly pull my hips back and then plunge back into her honeyed depths. Over and over, I pulsate into her, the only sound in the room our satisfied moans.

I kiss her again before sitting up. I look down at where we're joined, reach between us, and press a finger to her swollen clit. I pull her hips onto my legs, going deeper inside her, hitting her at an angle that floods her pussy.

I stroke her clit as I pump into her, and the orgasm hits her hard. She squeezes me like a vise, and I come, shooting my seed deep inside her womb. I'm panting, eyes open, watching her, waiting for regret to show on her face, but all I see is pure satisfaction.

I clench my eyes, hands hooked onto her waist, and lean my head back. "It was too fast… I—"

I let my voice trail off. I don't know what to say, but I do know it all happened too fast. If this is it for us, there's at least a hundred different things I would have wanted to do to her. I would have like to have tasted her one last time. Hell, I would have liked to have drawn it out for hours or days, and I still wouldn't have done everything I want to do with her.

"Lo…" Bree says, shortening my name with her breathy voice like she does.

I unclench my eyes and look down at her wincing face. "You're hurting me," she confesses.

In an instant, I unclench my hands from her hips. "Fuck, I'm sorry. I shouldn't…" I pull out of her and climb out of the bed.

Awkwardly, I walk into the bathroom to clean up. I come back with a hot towel and am surprised to see her standing next to the door. She avoids my gaze and walks into the bathroom, closing the door behind her.

I toss the towel into the hamper, pull my underwear and shorts back on, and sit on the edge of the bed. I should regret what just happened. Hell, I should probably get the hell out of here, but I don't want to do either of those things. I want to stay right here and hold her for the rest of the night.

Minutes later, she walks out of the bathroom with her robe wrapped around her. I hate that she's covered her body. "Hey—" I start and then pause. I'm not even sure what I want to say here.

She wraps her arms around herself and avoids looking at me. "I thought you would be gone."

It's like a kick in the gut. "What? You thought I'd get off and then get out?" I stand up, towering over her. "Is that what you think I'm doing here, Bree? You thought I wanted to fuck you so I would show up here, night after night, acting like I'm helping you, and then as soon as I get what I want, I'd leave?"

She opens her mouth to say something and then snaps it closed, shaking her head. Her voice is softer. "No, I know you're not like that, but I also know that you didn't really want that to happen."

I blurt out a laugh. "You thought I didn't want to fuck you?"

My harsh language has her wincing. She lowers her eyes to the floor. "I know I took advantage of the situation. You were trying to help me, and I—" She gestures to the bed. "Well, you know what happened next."

I take a step toward her, and we're so close that I can feel the rise and fall of her chest against mine. "You really think I didn't want that? You think that happened because you… what…?"

I blow out a breath and then shake my head. "Bree… baby… I've wanted you since I walked away from you. I wanted you even when I wanted to hate you. You are a temptation that I can't resist, and yeah, even though I'm sure there are a hundred reasons why us having sex is a bad idea, I don't regret it."

She leans her head back to look up at me. "You don't?"

I shake my head. Fuck, I have to find a way to move forward, but I don't know if I can ever fully forgive her. "I don't regret it. I don't think I could if I wanted to."

She puts her hands at my waist, and I suck in a breath. Her voice is soft and vulnerable. "So you're going to stay the night?"

"Yeah... to make sure the nightmares don't come back."

Even as I say it, I know it's a lie. I'm staying because there's no way I can walk out of here now. I don't reach for her like I want to. Instead, I take a step back and walk over to the bed and lie down.

She watches me for a minute, and when I pat the bed, she comes to lie down next to me. I reach for her, pulling her against my chest. "Sleep."

She nods and sighs as she leans into me. I wait for her to fall asleep before I hold her tighter and think about how I wish things could be different.

CHAPTER 12
BREE

I walk out of Sugar Bakery, cup of coffee in hand. It's Monday morning, and after spending the last few nights with Logan, I'm wondering what is going to happen today. Just like every other morning, he left before I woke up.

I walk into the office holding my breath but slowly exhale when I see the front area is empty. Logan's office door is closed, and I'm setting my stuff down on the desk when Alex walks in.

"Morning," he grunts.

I force a smile to my face. "Morning."

He disappears down the hall, and I sit down to work.

For the next few hours, I'm glancing at Logan's door what seems like every few minutes, but he never comes out. In the afternoon, I'm deep into spreadsheets when the front door opens and the mail carrier walks in.

The bell ringing over the door has me looking up. "Hey, Mark. How's it going today?"

He stops in front of my desk, and instead of handing me the mail, he holds it in front of him. "Good. Did you have a good weekend?"

I nod and try to hold back my blush because all I've been thinking about is Logan. "Yeah, it was good." He continues staring at me. "Uh, how was yours?"

He's smiling ear to ear now. "So, uh, Bree, I was wondering—"

Logan's door opening has both of us looking that way.

Logan walks out of his office and looks between Mark and me. He takes the mail from Mark's hands. "Thanks for bringing this in." He turns to me. "I need to see you in my office, please."

Stunned at his abruptness, I stand up, grabbing a notepad off my desk. "Thanks, Mark."

He nods. His smile falters for all of two seconds, and then he smiles again. "I'll see you later."

I nod and watch him leave. Sucking in a deep breath, I walk into Logan's office. I barely get inside before he demands, "Shut the door."

My eyebrows skyrocket up. He's standing behind his desk, hands in his pockets. I sort of expected the silent treatment that he's given me this morning, but I wasn't ready for this.

I turn and shut the door before walking farther into the room.

He gestures to the desk. "You can put the notepad down. You won't be taking any notes."

I set it down, back up a few feet, and then rub my hands together.

"What… what is this?"

He gestures with his head toward the lobby and my desk. "Does that happen a lot?"

I look at the wood door as if it holds all the answers, but I can't make any sense of his question. "Does what happen a lot?"

"The mailman?"

My forehead creases. "The mailman? What about him?"

Logan comes around his desk and then sits on the edge facing me. His jaw is tight, and he's staring at me as if he's looking through me. "Does he always come in and flirt with you?"

My eyes widen at his jealous tone. I blurt out a laugh. "He brings the mail in. He's not flirting with me."

He doesn't even smile. "Has he asked you out?"

I open my mouth and then snap it closed. My hesitation has him standing up and coming toward me. He stops a foot away, but I can feel the pulse in my body at just being closer to him. He tilts his head to the side. "Has he asked you out, Bree?"

I lift my chin. "Yeah… when I first started working here, he asked me out, but I told him no."

He slowly starts to walk around me and doesn't try to hide the fact that he's openly ogling me. His voice is husky when he replies, "It seems telling him no didn't work. He's still wanting you, wishing he could have you."

He's standing behind me, and I hear him lock the door. My breath comes out in a whoosh, and my whole body trembles. I just stand here, tense, anticipating what's about to happen.

He moves to stand behind me, and I can feel the warmth of his body, but he's still not touching me. "He wants you, Bree."

I clench my fists at my sides and arch my back as if I'm searching for his heat.

His voice is like a whisper in my ear. "He wants what I had last night."

And then suddenly what happened between us has turned ugly. I turn on him, unable to hide the anger. "What? You planning on pimping me out or something?"

Shock registers on his face, and then he shakes his head. His hands go to my hips, and I'm two seconds from pulling away from him when he drops a bombshell. "No. There's no fuckin' way I'd share you, Bree. I think you know that about me."

He pauses for a moment while I stare at him in shock. "I know men look at you," he finally goes on. "They can't help it. But they need to know that they can't have you. Not as long as we're... doing this."

I flip my head to look at him. "Doing what? I

thought these last few nights was a just a thing. I thought—"

I let my voice trail off. I need to let him speak because I'm tired of trying to guess what he's thinking.

He pulls my hips back so our lower bodies are pressed together. His hard manhood presses against my ass, and I lean into him. His arms circle me, holding me tighter to him. His hands are moving the whole time he's speaking to me.

"Thing?" he repeats with disgust. "You think I can work next to you, day after day, and not touch you?" His hands cup my breast, squeezing me. "Is that what you want?"

"Yes… No…" I answer, confused because I can't make sense of anything while he's touching me like this.

One hand travels down my body, and he pulls my skirt up so he can palm my panty-clad pussy. "You want me to touch you? Or you don't want me to touch you?"

He presses a finger over the sodden middle of my panties, pushing into me, and I arch into his hand. "I want you to touch me."

He slides his hand under the material, and as soon as the pad of his finger touches me, I feel that I'm going to explode. He chuckles in my ear. "You like that, don't you?"

I open my legs farther, giving him access, and he strokes me, coating his finger with my desire before strumming my clit. My head falls back against his shoulder, and he keeps stroking me, murmuring in my ear, "Does that feel good, baby? You like that?"

I can feel the orgasm brewing, and I clutch his arm. He chuckles, deep and throaty. "Give it to me, Bree. I want you to come on my hand, baby."

He kisses the side of my neck, and I go off, body writhing, every muscle pulled tight. He's relentless and doesn't slow down as my body no longer feels like my own. Over and over, he brings me over the edge, and after another orgasm, I'm lying limp and face down across his desk.

"Look at me," he demands.

I lift my head so I can look at him over my shoulder. He pulls his hand up and sucks my arousal off his fingers. His eyes close briefly, showing his enjoyment. It's like tasting me makes him unhinged.

Putting a hand to my back, he presses me into the desk. He pulls my skirt up over my ass, my panties down to my knees, and then stops.

The sound of his belt coming off, his zipper coming down, and his pants falling has me gripping the edge of the table.

His hands knead at my ass, and then he gives me a hard slap.

I whimper as he grabs my hips, his fingers digging into my skin. He pulls me back, and his bare manhood ruts along my clit. I'm too sensitive there, and I put my head down on the desk and force myself to breathe.

One hand leaves me, and I look at him over my shoulder. He grips his manhood, lining it up at my core. He slides into me, and I groan as he does it in one fluid motion, not stopping until he's completely filled me up.

He pauses, letting me adjust to him, and then slowly starts to pummel in and out of me.

I turn my head and groan into the hard wood. "Yes."

He plows into me, over and over, grunting.

He leans over, and with every plunge inside me, he grunts.

"He can look, but he can't touch you, Bree."

"I'm the only one that gets to see you like this."

"You're mine, baby. Just mine."

I'm not sure he even knows what he's saying. Every word out of his mouth is filled with possessiveness.

He drives into me harder and reaches around, putting a finger against my already sensitive nub. I shake my head. "I can't…"

He chuckles in my ear. "You don't think I can make you come again?"

I clench my eyes shut, and it's as if I'm fighting my own body because the sensation is there and my body is fully reacting to his touch. "I can't," I say again even as my body starts to succumb to the pressure.

He lifts me up and starts hitting me at another angle. There's no holding back, and I squeeze on to him tighter as the orgasm hits me fast and hard. I scream.

He turns my head and covers my mouth with his as my body writhes with the climax. He pummels into me until he's shot every drop of cum deep inside.

I wait for him to take back what he said. Or to say it was in the heat of the moment, but he says none of those things.

He pulls out of me but uses his finger to push his cum inside me and hold it there. "Mine, Bree. You're mine until I'm done with you."

I should hate him. I should tell him to go to hell or twenty other things, but I deserve this. I made him like this.

I watch him as he walks into his bathroom. He looks at me through the open door and beckons me to follow him.

I look on the floor around me and can't find my panties. I can feel the heat in my cheeks as I walk into the bathroom. "I can't find my underwear."

He pats his front pocket. "I have them."

He grabs a towel from under the sink and puts it under the spray of the warm water. I try to take it from him, but he doesn't let it go. "I got you."

He then proceeds to clean me up before taking care of himself.

I watch open-mouthed as he cleans himself up and then pulls my skirt fully down over my hips.

I hold a hand out. "And my underwear?"

He pats his pocket. "I'm keeping them."

I put my hands on my hips. "You want me to work without any panties on?"

He groans and shakes his head. "I didn't think this through."

He steps toward me and puts a finger under my chin, lifting my head so I have to look at him. "I won't get any work done knowing you are in there without any panties, but I'm keeping them." His voice softens. "You okay with everything? All I can give you is this until your contract is up."

I gulp hard. I want to tell him everything, but I don't know how he's going to react. At this point, I don't know if it's going to help matters or make them worse, so I keep my mouth shut and nod.

He tilts his head. "Talk to me, Bree. You're being too quiet."

I tell him honestly, "I'll take whatever you'll give me, Logan. I know that makes me sound desperate and well, frankly, not very smart, but it's the truth.

If you're willing to be with me for the next several months, I'll take it."

He leans down and seals his lips over mine. The kiss is intense, and when his tongue slides along mine, I whimper.

He breaks the kiss and stares into my eyes. "I'm just as desperate for you, Bree."

I pull from his hold and put some distance between us. "So, uh, how is this going to work? Are we keeping this between us? No one needs to know... or uh, what are you thinking?"

I prepare myself because I'm sure he doesn't want to announce to the town that he's with his ex-girlfriend. He raises his eyebrows. "What? You think I'd treat you like a booty call? Is that what you're thinking?"

I just stare at him. "I don't know what to think. I know you don't want to hear this... hell, you probably don't even believe it, but I came here to try and fix us."

He holds his hand up. "There's no fixing us, Bree. We don't have a future together, not like that. We can uh, enjoy each other, but there's an end to it."

He's going to break my heart. That's all I'm making out of what he's saying.

He reaches for my hand and threads our fingers together. "But no, I'm not going to hide this. As far as people need to know, we're dating. That's all."

I roll my eyes at him. "This is Whiskey Run. I've only been here a few months, but even I know that the rumor mills are going to be busy with this."

He shrugs. "I don't care what people think. As long as the two of us know what this is, that's all that matters."

I bite my tongue and nod my head.

He lifts my hand up and kisses my knuckles. "Now we'd probably better get back to work."

I nod and back away. I grab my notepad that was pushed to the floor and then go to unlock his door. He stops me. "And Bree—"

I turn and look at him. "Yeah?"

His voice is strained. "As long as we're doing this, you're mine. If you decide you want to be with someone else, you just need to be upfront and tell me."

I open my mouth to argue with him. He still thinks I cheated on him, and I didn't. Not like he thinks. Before I can get anything out, he walks over to his desk, sits down, and picks up his phone, dismissing me.

I wish I could tell him that I love him and I never stopped loving him, but he obviously doesn't want to hear it. I walk out of his office, happy and sad at the same time. Happy that I get to be with him but sad that he's already planning the end.

CHAPTER 13
LOGAN

This week has flown by. I adjust my tie in the bathroom mirror at work. Tonight is the night of the fundraiser, and I should have already been out the door. Bree left hours ago because she joined some committee to help with setup.

I can barely contain myself, excited to spend the evening with her. I've been a little on edge, and I've discovered it's because I want the whole town to know she's taken, and after tonight, they won't have any doubt.

My phone rings, and when I see my brother's name, I answer. "Hey, Penn! What's up?"

He's loudly whispering into the phone, "Where the fuck are you?"

My brother, the doctor, handles everything with ease, and nothing ever gets him rattled, so to hear him upset has me on high alert. "I'm at the office, why?"

In another hushed whisper, he says, "Because I'm here at the fundraiser with your date, and Aria didn't come, so everyone thinks that I'm here with Katie. I'm telling you, Logan, you have five minutes to get here or I'm never fixing you up again."

As soon as what he's saying hits me, I know I fucked up. I completely forgot that my brother had arranged a date for me. "Fuck!" I scream and then again for good measure, I say it again. "Fuck!"

Penn is calmer now. "Logan, it's fine, just get here."

I'm already out the door. I lock it behind me, and with a rushed ramble, I tell him, "Oh my God, Penn, listen to me. Do not, I mean, do not, introduce Katie to Bree."

The silence on the other end of the line is telling.

"Penn… did you hear me?"

"I thought you and Bree had broken up."

I'm rushing down the sidewalk toward the

community center. "Penn, we were, but we're not now. Just keep them apart."

I hang up the phone and start running. I'm not sure how I'm going to handle this, but I have to do something. I see my other brother about to walk in the community center, and I scream his name. "Miller!"

He turns to look, and I wave like a maniac. I sprint toward him. "I need a favor." I'm huffing and puffing. "Please, I'm begging you."

He chuckles, shaking his head. "What do you need?"

I grab his upper arms. "I have two dates tonight. I need you to take one of them."

He chuckles and runs his hand through his scruffy beard. "You have two dates… why don't you just keep them both? Most women wouldn't mind sharing a Brody brother—hell, they may get off on it."

I shake my head, squeezing his arms even tighter. "I don't want to date them both. Look, I forgot Penn was setting me up, and I'm seeing Bree—"

"Your ex? I thought you two broke up."

I growl. "Look, there's no time. I'm seeing Bree, and she's going to be pissed already. Can you help me out with this Katie?"

Miller puts his hand on my shoulder. "I can't. I'm seeing someone."

My mouth drops open. "What? You mean today, right, like a one-night stand or something because you never 'date,' not seriously anyway."

His forehead creases. "No, not a one-night stand. I want to date her, but…"

His voice trails off, and I gasp, "But what?"

He growls. "She won't go out with me."

I shake my head in amazement. "What? You're telling me that Miller Brody, billionaire, got turned down?"

He grimaces. "Fuck you, Logan. If you want my help, this is not the way to go about it."

I grip his arms again. "Fuck, I'm sorry. Please, I'm begging you. Can you help me… just for tonight?"

He rolls his eyes. "Fine. But you owe me."

I throw an arm around his shoulder. "I'm not sure

what I can do for you, but yeah, whatever, man. I got you."

As soon as we walk in the door, I spot Bree. She is standing with all of my brothers and my sister and of course a woman that I'm assuming is Katie. My brother, Ozzy, has his cowboy hat on and sticks out like a sore thumb. There's a crowd around Guy, most likely congratulating him on his team making it to the playoffs. My sister, Skyler, is hovering next to Bree protectively, staring daggers at me. Fuck me. This can't be my life.

My brother Penn sees me and instantly looks relieved.

I slow my steps, looking between Bree and the other woman.

Bree knows. It's obvious by the pained look on her face. Hell, it seems my whole family has it figured out because they're all giving me dirty looks. I stop next to Bree and put my hand at the small of her back, but she pulls away from me. She talks to my sister Skyler, completely ignoring me. "I'm going to go see if anyone needs anything."

I blow out a breath as I go to Penn and gesture to the woman. "Hi, you must be Katie. I'm Logan. Can we talk for a minute?"

I step away from my family, tugging Miller with me, and I can feel Bree staring. I fucked up, and I can't blame her if she never talks to me again.

"Look, uh, Katie, I'm not sure how to say this. I forgot that my brother arranged a date for me tonight, and I seem to have double-booked."

She stares at me in shock. "You have two dates?"

I nod. "Yes, and I'm sorry, I should have canceled, but—"

She points to herself. "You mean with me?"

I nod. "Yeah, see, Bree and I have a history, and—"

She holds her hand up. "Look, no worries. I mean, it's a douche move, but—"

I can't even blame her for being pissed. "Anyway, this is my brother Miller, and he would love to be your date for the night if that's okay with you."

She looks stunned and gestures between Miller and me. "What? So you decided to pimp me out to your brother?"

I put both hands up. "No, of course not. I just didn't want you to spend the evening alone, that's all."

Miller gives me a look, and I know that when he asks for paybacks, I'm going to have to ante up because this is quickly turning into a headache. I blow out a breath. "Look, I really am sorry. I know this is bad, and I have no excuse except that I forgot that Penn set us up. You seem lovely, but—"

She shrugs and looks at Miller. "Do you dance?"

He gives me a look, and I know if we were alone, he'd be cussing me out right about now. "Yeah, I can dance."

She looks Miller up and down, and even I can see the dollar signs in her eyes. Miller may be covered in tattoos, but he's obviously well off. His suit is designer, and the man just screams money. "You'll do." She shrugs.

I put my hand on Miller's shoulder. "Thanks, brother. See you two at the table."

I turn and go in search of Bree. I see her across the room, talking to my sister. I almost reach them, but as soon as she spots me, she practically runs from the room without a backward glance.

I'm about to chase after her when my little sister steps in front of me, blocking my path. "Are you fuckin' kidding me?"

I'm in trouble. If Skyler is cussing, I'm definitely in trouble. "Look, I know I fucked up, but I'm trying to fix it."

She crosses her arms over her chest and taps her foot. "Really? You're going to fix it?" She leans toward me, and it would have more effect if she were taller. "So you didn't plan this to get back at her?"

I shake my head. "To get back at her? You mean at Bree?"

She nods. "Yes! I'm not sure what that means, but that's what Bree thinks, and so help me Logan, if you did this on purpose—"

I cut her off. "Sis, you know me, I would never do something like this on purpose. Now please, can I go fix this?"

She uncrosses her arms and puts her hands on her hips. "You better fix this, Logan Brody, because I like her, and the woman obviously loves you and—"

"I'll take care of it."

I'm letting Skyler's words surround me as I walk through the door that Bree walked through. She's walking out of the ladies' room, and when she sees me, her jaw tenses, and she stops. Fuck, she's beautiful. Her red dress clings to every curve of her body. Her hair is up in some kind of knot, and she's got tendrils hanging down. Her lipstick matches her dress, and I want to kiss it off her, right here, in front of everyone.

People are walking up and down the hall, mostly ignoring us, but it wouldn't take much for us to become the main attraction.

She crosses her arms over her chest, pushing her cleavage up. I would gape at her if I thought it wouldn't piss her off even more. "Bree, listen—"

She stops me with a sharp laugh. "I don't need to listen. I hear you, loud and clear. I get it."

She tries to walk away, but I stop her by holding her shoulders. She jerks from me and huskily whispers, "Don't touch me, Logan Brody."

I hold my hands up. People are starting to stare, and I look around. There's a small conference room just a few feet away. "Look, give me two minutes."

She shakes her head. "No."

Desperation hits me hard. "Bree, baby, please, you have to believe me, I didn't plan this. I would never do something like this and—"

She taps her foot. "So you didn't plan a date with two women tonight?"

I wince. Fuck, it sounds bad when she says it. "Listen…" I take a step toward her but don't reach for her like I want to. I gesture to the door off to the side. "There's a conference room right there. Please, just hear me out."

She walks away from me, and I'm about to beg again, but she stops outside the conference room door. "Two minutes."

She breezes into the room, and I follow.

I have to fix this. I have to.

CHAPTER 14
BREE

I'm so upset I'm shaking.

I'm embarrassed, and I don't know what to do with that. I've never been in this situation before, and all the pitying looks from Logan's siblings is enough to make me want to leave Whiskey Run and not come back.

But I have responsibilities. I volunteered my help for tonight, and I can't just walk away. Even when Katie was introduced to me as Logan's date, it was obvious he hadn't told any of his siblings we were dating or somewhat together, but Skyler knew by the look on my face, and she must have told the others.

I look down at my shoes. "Just say it, Logan. Just tell me whatever it is you want to tell me so I can go home.

He closes the door behind him and comes to stand in front of me. I hold my hand up, not wanting him to come any closer because I don't trust myself with him. Even now, when he's broken my heart and embarrassed me, I don't trust myself to not fall at his feet. He frowns at me. "Bree, listen to me, please. The first day I was back in town, I talked to my brother, Penn. He knew that it was hard for me to be back at work and seeing you every day. He knew how I felt about you."

I lift my eyes to look at him but keep my guard up.

He continues, "He said he would arrange a date for me tonight and, uh, I said okay."

I take a step back. "So you did have two dates tonight? It wasn't some kind of misunderstanding?"

Instead of answering me, he shakes his head. "I forgot all about it. He didn't say anything else, and neither did I. After this week, I wasn't thinking about anything but me and you."

I suck in a breath. "So you didn't plan this on purpose… to hurt me?"

He reaches for me, and this time I don't pull away. He puts his hands on my bare shoulders. "I would never do something like that to hurt you. I don't want to hurt you, Bree. I couldn't."

I tilt my head to the side. "Even after… our past… and what happened between us?"

He winces like he can't stand the memory, and I completely get where he's coming from. I hate thinking about that part of our past too.

He brings a hand up and cups my jaw. "Bree, I would never intentionally hurt you. You have to believe me. This was an accident, pure and simple. I talked to Katie and explained the situation. Miller is going to be her date tonight, and I'm going to owe him big time for that, but it doesn't matter. I was looking forward to being with you. I want you on my arm. I want all of Whiskey Run to know that you are mine."

Now is probably not the time, but I tilt my chin at him. "You mean… for the next nine months?"

"We should talk about that. I don't know if I can ever forget what happened but—"

I put my hands at his waist. "I listened to you; now it's your turn to listen to me."

He tenses, and I pull him by his jacket so that we're flush against each other. "Tonight, when it's just the two of us, I want you to hear me out. I need to explain…"

He doesn't want to. His lips turn down, and he's already shaking his head, but I have to get him to hear me out. "Logan, listen to me. We both know that we want more than something temporary. We were talking about marriage and—"

He cuts me off. "That was before…"

His voice trails off, and something inside me says not to give in. Not this time. "Look, let's have our night out. We'll dance, eat, have a good time. Then we'll go back to my apartment and talk. If after tonight, you don't forgive me, I'll leave. I won't hold you to the contract I signed with Zach. I'll just go."

My heart breaks at the thought of leaving Logan, but I know I'll have to. A temporary thing with him would not be temporary for me. My heart is all in, and the longer we're together, the harder this will be when it ends.

I can't make sense of the look on his face.

"Please, Logan…"

He pulls me against his chest and wraps his arms around me. "Okay, we'll talk later." His chest expands as he takes a deep breath in. "We'll talk afterward. But now I want to enjoy tonight with you."

He pulls back and releases me. "Let's do this over." He clears his throat. "Bree, you're so fuckin' beautiful you take my breath away."

My heart does a flip in my chest. I feel like I've been on a roller coaster of emotions. "And you're looking pretty handsome yourself, Lo."

He drags me to him again, holding me close, like he doesn't want to let me go. "Do you forgive me?"

How can I not? I do believe him; I don't have any reason not to. "I forgive you, but just so you know, I don't like to share either, Logan. If there's any part of you that wants to be on a date with... her... then just tell me now."

He kisses the top of my head. "I don't. I want you... only you."

He holds his hand out, and I put mine in it. He threads our fingers together and pulls me from the conference room. We walk down the hall, back into the party room, and we both keep looking and smiling at each other.

Everyone is at their seats now, and he pulls out a chair for me to sit at. We're surrounded by his family. Some of them are at the next table, but at our table is Penn, an empty seat next to him, Miller, and then Katie is seated next to me. I suck in a breath. "Hi, I'm Bree."

I prepare myself for the worst. I can't blame the woman if she's mad about tonight, but she seems to have taken it all in stride. She leans toward me. "I'm Katie, and I have to say, I don't blame Logan at all. You're beautiful."

My face heats up. "You're beautiful. I'm sorry about all this."

She waves me off. "Are you kidding? I work all the time, so this has been an adventure for me. At least I've had something exciting happen."

"What do you do?" I ask her as I take in Miller's tense stature. He's aloof, but I've never known him to be uncomfortable, and I don't know what to make of it. Of course, I've only been around him a few times, but the way he's looking right now doesn't add up with all the stories Logan has told me about him.

Katie brings me back when she points at Penn. "I'm a nurse at the hospital with Penn."

We talk a little about her job, and when there's a lull in the conversation, Logan asks Penn, "Where's Aria tonight? I thought for sure she'd be here. She loves this kind of thing."

Penn nods without smiling. "She does love this kind of thing."

The look he's giving Logan says not to ask more. I met Aria years ago, and I've seen her a few times since I've been in Whiskey Run. There's obviously something going on there, but I'm not in a place to ask. Whatever it is, the whole table is affected by it. Miller and Logan are both looking at their brother. They want to ask questions, but neither of them does.

Logan slides his hand into my lap and holds my hand.

He squeezes it, and I look at him as he whispers, "You okay?"

I nod. "Yeah, I'm good."

After a rough start, the rest of the night goes off without a hitch. We eat, we dance, and Logan doesn't let me leave his side the whole night. It's almost time to go when he whispers in my ear, "Come home with me."

I lift my eyes to his. "You want me to come to your house?"

He nods, and I can't help but feel this is something big. I have to remind myself that tonight is the night we're having the talk. Tonight could essentially be our last night together.

I nod. "Okay."

"Did you walk here?"

I shake my head. "No, since I had to bring all my stuff and get ready here, I drove."

He nods. "You want your car at my house? Or I can bring you back here tomorrow to get it."

I bite my lip as I think about it. If I leave my car here, there's going to be speculation that I've gone home with Logan. But if I park my car in his driveway, then the whole town will know I'm spending the night with him. I tilt my head to the side. "Can I park in your driveway?"

His jaw tightens, and he cups my cheek. "We don't have to hide-—"

I nod with a blink. "I know, but let's see what happens tonight and then-—"

He chuckles. "I know exactly what's going to happen tonight. As soon as we get behind closed doors, you're mine."

I lean into him. I love how much he wants me, and it seems he's not able to control it. "Sounds good."

CHAPTER 15
LOGAN

I pull Bree into my side and am about to find the nearest exit. We ate, we danced, and I made the decision that I want her at my house, in my life, and with me period. This is not something temporary. I was a fool to think that was even possible. I'm going to hear her out, and then I'm going to find it within myself to forgive her, forget the past, and build a future with her.

Tonight when I thought I'd fucked up and that I might lose her, I knew right then that I couldn't imagine my life without her in it.

I point at the closest exit, and Bree puts a hand to my chest. "Hold up there. We can't just leave."

I chuckle and wrap my arms around her. "Yes, we

can. Look, people are already leaving. We sure can walk right out of here."

She smiles up at me. "Logan, your family is still here. We should at least say goodbye."

I blow out a breath. I'm impatient, ready to get Bree alone, but I know she's right. "Okay. We'll say goodbye, and then we're out of here."

She giggles. "You sure are in a hurry."

I clench her waist and pull her flush against me. "Yeah, I am. I'm tired of sharing you."

She rolls her eyes, but I can tell my words please her. She pats me on the chest. And automatically, I pull my shoulders back, puffing out my chest. Fuck, it feels good to have her in my arms. "Let's go say goodbye to everyone."

We walk toward the tables where my family was, and Bree points to the dance floor. "There's Guy!"

I try to see around the people on the dance floor, and Bree laughs. "Right there, where the group of women are dancing."

I roll my eyes. "Yeah, same ol' Guy. I'll catch up with him later."

I no sooner get the words out and Ozzy walks up to me. His cowboy hat is still sitting on the top of his head, and he is wearing the scowl that seems to be a permanent feature for him. "Hey, Ozz."

He grunts. "I came. I'm leaving now."

I tilt my head to the side. Ozzy is even grumpier than usual. "Everything okay?"

He nods. "Yep, everything is good. See you, brother." He tips his hat to Bree. "See you, Bree."

As soon as Ozzy walks away, Bree turns to me. "Something is off with him, right? Or is that just Ozzy?"

I look at Ozzy's retreating back. His wife died a few years ago, and he hasn't been the same since. But he's taking his grumpiness to a whole new level.

I blow out a breath as Skyler and Zach walk up to us. "We're getting out of here."

I nod, pulling Bree to my side. "Us too."

My sister asks Bree, "You okay?"

Bree leans into me. "Yeah, I'm okay."

As they leave, I look around for Miller, but he's nowhere to be found. Ready to get Bree to myself, I pull her with me toward the door. "Come on. I'll catch up with Miller later."

A few people stop us on the way out, and by the time we get outside, I'm going crazy. There's a need inside of me that I can't tamp down. It's like I need to tell Bree right now that the past doesn't matter and I want to be with her no matter what.

We finally get out the door, and Bree points to my brother. "There's Miller."

He's talking on his phone, and the closer we get, the more conversation we can hear. "Lindsey, listen, I wasn't on a date with anyone."

He jams his hand in his hair. "I know it looks bad, but if you let me explain—"

He holds the phone out and stares at it, and it's obvious that he was hung up on. Shit. I really fucked this up.

I'm wrestling with the fact I want to get Bree home and guilt for what I did to my brother. It's my fault he was on a date tonight, and obviously he's paying for it. With remorse, I look at Bree. "I should go talk to him."

She nods. "Yeah, how about I go to my apartment—"

Before she gets it all out, I hook my arm around her waist. "You're staying at my house."

She goes to her tiptoes and loops her arms around my neck, pressing her breasts against my chest. "I know I am. I'm going to pack a bag, and when you're done here, you can pick me up."

I reluctantly nod. I don't want to be away from her, but I really do need to talk to Miller. "Okay. Please drive carefully and I'll be there in a few minutes."

She giggles and points down the street. "Logan… You can literally see my apartment from here. What do you think is going to happen?"

I blow out a breath and look into her eyes. It's on the tip of my tongue to tell her I love her when Miller calls my name.

I clench my eyes shut and shake my head. "I'm sorry. I gotta deal with this… I'll be there soon."

She nods. "Yeah, I'll be ready."

She turns to walk away, but I grab her around the waist and pull her to me. I kiss her with the weight of everything I feel. She leans into me, and I cup her face, deepening the kiss and swiping my tongue along hers. She moans, and I break off with a huffed breath. "I'll be there to pick you up soon. Pack clothes for the whole weekend."

Her eyebrows lift, but she nods her head. Reluctantly, I let her walk away and then go over to my brother. He's sitting on the curb, and he's ditched the jacket and rolled up his sleeves, baring his tattooed arms. He's lost in thought, rubbing his hand through the scruff of his beard. Anyone passing him on the street right now wouldn't know he was a billionaire.

As soon as he sees me coming, his eyes glint, and he glares at me.

"I'm sorry."

He shakes his head. "I should have known that someone would post pictures on FriendSpace."

I sit on the curb next to him, and when he doesn't say anything else, I piece it together. "Someone posted pictures of you with Katie, and the woman you like saw it."

He winces as he lifts his phone up. He opens a text, makes the image full screen and points the screen at me. "Yeah, she sent me a text with the picture." He gestures to the image. It's him and Katie, and they're dancing close together. I grimace. "Yeah, that's not good."

His jaw tightens. "No shit. It's definitely not good. I thought I was making headway and she was finally trusting me, but all that has been ruined at this point."

I turn toward him. "You really like this girl."

He gapes at me. "I told you I did. I fucked up."

"Did you tell her you were helping me out?"

He laughs. "She wouldn't listen. She didn't want to hear it."

I blow out a breath. "Let her cool off and then talk to her."

"What if she doesn't listen? What if I blew it?"

I tilt my head at my brother. He's always been confident, hell, almost arrogant, so seeing him like this is strange.

I shake my head. "You're Miller Brody! THE Miller Brody, and I know you. You'll find a way to make her listen, and if it's meant to be between the two of you, you'll be together."

I expect to see that determined look on his face, but he just shrugs. "Yeah, I guess."

I rest my elbow on my knee and put my chin in my hand. "Well, all I know is I can't wait to meet her. Finally, some woman that doesn't fall for your charm—"

He interrupts me. "My money, you mean?"

I nod. "Money, charm… all I'm saying is I wanna meet her. I've never seen you like this before."

He blows out a rough breath. "I've never felt this way before."

I'm torn. I want to go pick up Bree, but I know Miller needs me. I've never seen him like this. So I settle back, put my hands on the sidewalk, and ask, "Tell me about her."

And he starts to talk.

For fifteen minutes, Miller talks about the woman that he obviously loves. I keep looking at my watch, ready to go, but I force myself to sit here and listen. I owe him that at least.

CHAPTER 16
BREE

I push the code into the door at Savage Ink with a smile on my face. I'm nervous, but I'm excited about what the night holds. I practically run up the stairs, which is no small feat in my heels. As I get to the top, an uneasy feeling comes over me, but I ignore it and unlock my door. I set my purse and bag down and look around the empty room.

Shaking off the uneasy feeling, I take off my shoes as I walk down the hall to my bedroom. I change from my dress to a pair of jeans and a T-shirt. I walk into the bathroom to pack my toiletry bag and stop when I see the writing on the mirror.

"Found you!" is scrawled on the mirror with red lipstick.

My heart drops in my chest, and I start to panic. That uneasy feeling is back tenfold. I start to sweat, my heart starts to race, and my body starts to tremble. I'm not alone. The thought hits me, and before I can turn around, scream, or run, an arm comes around me, and a big hand covers my mouth. I see us in the mirror. I'm shocked, eyes round, and the man behind me doesn't even attempt to hide from me. Piercing ice blue eyes stare back at me. *John. The man that I kissed. The man that has made my life a living hell these last two years.*

I struggle against his hold, but he's not relenting. He drags me from the room, down the hallway, and to the front door. I know I can't let him take me out of here, so I fight like I've never fought before. I jerk my body in different directions, clawing at his hands and fighting as hard as I can.

His voice is demanding in my ear. "Stop it, Bree or else I'm going to stay here and wait for your little boyfriend to show up and kill him right in front of you."

My whole body goes limp. Logan will be here any minute, and even though John is no match for him, Logan won't be ready for something like this. I can't put him in this situation. I can't believe I brought

John and his Mafia family right to Whiskey Run. Right to Logan.

John smirks at me. "I'm guessing you don't want me to meet your new boyfriend, do you?"

I pull from his hold, and this time he lets me go. I hold my hands up. "I'll go with you. Can I at least put my shoes on?"

I gesture beside the door where my tennis shoes are sitting.

He grunts. "Yes, but hurry."

As I'm putting on the tennis shoes, I ask him, "How did you find me?"

He shrugs. "It wasn't hard."

I shake my head. I did everything I could. I waited until the court proceedings were over. I emptied out my checking and savings. Paid cash for my move to Whiskey Run, and when I got here, I confessed to Zach, and he said he could seal my employment records. I have no idea how John found me, and I guess it doesn't matter now. I stand up and point at the door. "Lead the way."

He crosses his arms over his chest. "Leave your phone."

I point to my purse. "It's in there."

He pulls a gun from his waistband. "Any problems, I shoot. I wanted to come kill you. My dad thought you deserved to be tortured."

I hide my face from him, looking down at the ground as I walk out the door. I don't want him to see the fear I know is evident on my face. John's father, Luca, is the mob boss of the Antonelli family. I never wanted to get mixed up in any of this, but I didn't have much of a choice. It all just fell into my lap.

"How is your dad doing?" I ask, and even I'm surprised by how calm I sound.

John grabs my arm, digging his fingers into my skin. "He's serving a life sentence in a maximum security prison. How do you think he's doing?"

He walks me over to his truck, opens the passenger side door, and shoves me inside. He leans over me, glaring. "My father is an old man, and—"

I cut him off because there's no way I can sit here and listen to him spout about his father like he's a good man. "He was trafficking women. He was—"

I don't get the next words out. His fist connects with my face, and the pain is excruciating. He slams the door and stalks around to the driver's side. He's angry, and he drives erratically through town. I'm holding my hand to my face, wiping the blood from my split lip. "Where are we going?"

"Have you not learned anything? Just keep your mouth shut."

I stare out the window, watching the town go by, and when he pulls into the airstrip, I sit up a little taller. I've never been on the property, but this is where Logan worked when he was with the Ghost Team. I just know someone here will help me.

As if John can read my mind, he laughs. "Forget it. No one is going to rescue you."

He drives right up to a waiting airplane. He pulls me from the car, and I try to run, but I don't get far. John grabs me and drags me up the stairs to the airplane. Someone from the ground starts yelling, but the sound is gone when the door of the airplane closes. "We gotta go," John yells.

Instantly, the plane starts moving, and John slams me into a seat. "Stay put. Don't move. Don't say a fuckin' word… and I might make this a little less painful for you."

I close my eyes and lean my head back against the seat. My mind instantly goes to Logan. I would give anything to have told him I truly do love him and for him to believe it. Now I'll never be able to tell him. I'm going to die, and he's always going to believe that I cheated on him.

My head jerks back as the plane picks up speed. I look out the window, and there are police cars with their lights and sirens on, driving toward us. John goes to stand by the cockpit. "Get this thing in the air."

Almost instantly, we're in flight, and I turn to look as we leave Whiskey Run behind us.

I hear the pilot yelling over the roar of the engine. "I told you that when I landed there, I couldn't stay long. You don't know Walker."

John throws his hand up. "Fuck this Walker guy. I'm an Antonelli. No one can touch me. I'm not scared of some small town mercenary."

The pilot screams, "You should be."

John pulls his gun from his pants and points it at the pilot. I suck in a breath. Oh my God, he's going to kill him, and we're all going down.

John's voice is deep and lethal. "Talk to me like that again. I'm the boss here now. I'm the one in charge. Do you have a problem with that?"

"No," I hear the man murmur.

John stands there, holding the gun to the man's head, and I don't take a breath until he finally pulls it back and shoves it in his waistband. "Good. So land us in New York. I'm going to have some fun with her before the torture begins."

My stomach rolls, and I can feel the bile rising in my throat. I clench the arm rests and stare daggers at John.

I know what he plans to do me once we land, and I'm not going to let it happen. I will die fighting him off. I know he hates me for what I did. My testimony put his father in prison forever, and there is no way he's going to just let me live.

I close my eyes and take big breaths. A plan, that's what I need. And no matter how much I want someone to save me, I hope Logan stays far away from the Antonelli family because they're not going to like anything—or anyone—getting in their way.

CHAPTER 17
LOGAN

I'm smiling as I get out of my truck. I look up at the light of Bree's bedroom window and jog across the street to the downstairs apartment door. I push in the code to open the door and take the stairs two at a time, ready to get to Bree.

As soon as I get to the top, I see that her apartment door is wide open.

Not cracked. Not ajar. It's wide fucking open.

I frown but quickly shake it off, trying to explain it to myself. She knew I was coming. She left the door open for me.

I walk in and look around the empty living room. I don't even have to holler for her, I know she's not here. I've always thought I had some kind of sixth sense or something, but I call her name out anyway. "Bree?"

I walk through the apartment calling her name. Maybe she's visiting a neighbor, I think, but that's quickly squashed when I walk into the bathroom and see the writing on the mirror.

Found you. I stand staring at the mirror as my skin starts to crawl. No! What does this mean? Fuck, I should have made her tell me what happened to her and why she was having nightmares.

I walk through her bedroom and the rest of her apartment, looking for any clues. My phone dings, and it's an emergency text from the Ghost Team. I'm still on their call list, but it's only for Whiskey Run. I read the text. *911.Unknown plane on airstrip.*

I ignore the text and call Zach.

I'm pacing the living room as I wait for him to answer. I spot Bree's purse and open it. Her phone and wallet are still in there. Gripping her phone in my hand, I'm about to open it when Zach answers.

"What's up?"

"Zach. Bree's gone. I came to her apartment to pick her up, and she's gone."

He starts to talk. "Maybe she's at the neighbors or—"

I cut him off. "No! Someone wrote on her bathroom mirror, 'Found you.'" I huff out a breath. "I don't know who or what—"

Zach sighs. "Fuck, I do." I can hear my sister talking in the background, but Zach asks, "Are you still at her apartment?"

I set down her purse and phone. "Yeah, why?"

"I'll be there in three minutes. We're just around the corner."

With one last look around the apartment, I jog down the steps. I peek my head into Savage Ink. "Hey, Aiden! You seen Bree?"

He shakes his head. "No, why? What's up?"

I walk into the room. "She's gone, and I think someone took her. Did you ever put the security app on your phone?"

Aiden lays down his tattoo gun, eyes wide. "What the fuck? Yeah, I did." He pulls his phone from his pocket.

I stop next to him. "I need to see the last thirty minutes."

He's opening the app. "I knew they would find her."

My blood freezes. "Who?" I demand.

He stops the app at the image of some strange man manhandling Bree—my Bree—out the door.

Aiden holds the phone up to me. "You don't give testimony on the Mafia and just get away with it. I knew they would find her, I just hoped—"

I shake my head, confused. "I don't know what you're talking about."

Aiden looks at me, dumbfounded. "What? How could you—"

He's cut off when Zach comes in the door. "Logan! Let's go." I know that tone, and I know not to question him. He's always been determined, and he's got that edge to him right now. He's found out something.

I point at Aiden. "Send me that picture."

I'm calling out my phone number to Aiden as I run out the door.

Zach is running to my truck. "Skyler drove my truck home. Come on, we gotta go. Wheels up in ten minutes."

I get into the truck. "Ghost Team?"

He nods, and I start driving. "Zach, tell me what the fuck is going on. What do you know?"

Zach has one hand on the dash as I speed toward the facility. I look over at him. "Tell me everything you know about Bree. I have to find her."

He blows out a breath. "The guys are tracking her. She's in a plane, and we're assuming they're on their way to New York."

"With who? Why did Aiden say something about the Mafia?"

My friend looks at me with pure pity, and that's when I know how bad this is. "The Antonellis are the biggest crime family in New York. Come on, Lo, think. How many times have we—"

I cut him off. "What? The Antonelli family? They have my Bree? What is this? Some kind of revenge?"

Zach shakes his head. "No. Well, yes, it is but not what you're thinking. It's revenge on Bree, not you. Bree is the one that brought them down."

I gasp. The Antonellis are dangerous. They don't care about anyone but themselves. Just knowing what I do about them makes me sick to my stomach. I spit out the words. "What the fuck are you talking about?"

He points at the airstrip in front of us. I see some of my friends that are retired and work at the rehabilitation center standing at the bottom of the stairs to the plane.

We jog from the truck over to them. Zach slaps hands with his brother-in-law, Davis. "Thanks for being here, brother."

He nods. "Always."

Elias is holding his laptop to his chest. Colter and Kanan are already walking up the stairs to the plane.

It's not until we're inside and the door is closed that I start to ramble. "Now tell me what the hell you're talking about. What does Bree have to do with the Antonelli family?"

The guys all avoid my gaze, except for Zach. When he doesn't say anything, I demand, "How do you know that Bree was on a plane that flew out of here?"

Zach lifts his chin. "At 2200, a plane landed here.

Two minutes later, a car drove up, and the man forced a woman from the car onto the plane."

Davis holds his phone out to me, and I see Bree, frightened, being pushed up the stairs of the plane. My hands clench to fists.

I look at Zach. "What do they want with her?"

His voice is husky. "I don't know how to say this—"

"Just say it," I demand.

He nods. "Okay. Two years ago, she was consulting for the federal security system in New York."

I nod. I knew that. That's what she was doing when I met her. But that was her job. She helped companies get organized. "Okay," I say slowly, still not understanding.

He threads his fingers together in his lap. "When federal security found out that John Antonelli, the son of Luca Antonelli, was interested in Bree, they asked her to help build a case against them."

My eyes widen. "What the fuck? Did she not realize how dangerous—"

He cuts me off. "She heard that women were being trafficked, and she knew she had to help. She found the place where the women were being held, and she saved thirty women and children from being trafficked. Thirty, Logan!"

I stare back at him. "That's the guy I saw her with, isn't it? The one I thought she was cheating on me with?"

He nods solemnly.

"Fuck," I grunt, running my fingers through my hair. "Okay, so what's the plan?"

Elias looks up from his laptop. "We are thirty minutes behind them. I was able to track Bree's smart ring." He looks up at me. "As long as it remains active, we will know where she is."

My stomach clenches. "Okay. Okay, that's good."

Davis chimes in. "I'm sure they're taking her to the Antonellis' compound. We already have boots on the ground surrounding the area—"

I cut him off. "But—"

Davis shakes his head. "It's okay. They're our guys. They know the priority for this mission is Bree's safety."

As we get close to New York, guns and armor are being passed around. We're all loaded down with everything and anything we might need. I'm standing by the door, waiting to land, when we start to descend.

We walk off the plane, and there are multiple vehicles waiting for us. I know this was a lot to coordinate, but I'll never underestimate what Walker and his Ghost Team can do.

Zach points to the truck in front. "That's us."

We get in, and with directions from Elias, Zach takes off down the road. The three other SUVs are following us, and all I can do is sit here and pray that Bree is okay. I know she'll fight. I just hope she knows that I'm coming for her. I've held back. I've been unforgiving. And I would give anything for her to know that I love her and that I always have.

"Elias," I say softly.

He knows what I want to know without me even asking. He looks down at his laptop. "We're right behind them. We're still tracking her."

Davis reads a text from his phone. "They are in the compound. Our guys have taken out the men on the outside. They want to know if we want them to go in."

Davis looks at me, and I look to Elias. "How far away are we?"

He looks at his computer. "Eight minutes."

I clench my eyes and shake my head. "Davis. Tell them…"

Davis shakes his head. "They heard screaming. They're going in."

I nod. "Step on it, Zach."

The already speeding car takes off, and I stare out into the darkness. Eight minutes feels like forever, and I know that when I get to Bree and find her safe—because there is no other option—I won't ever let her out of my sight again.

CHAPTER 18
BREE

My head is hurting, my lip is busted and swollen, and I'm about to give up all hope when there's a loud boom, and then all I can see is smoke. I roll away from John and against the wall. I'm in the fetal position, head held down and praying I don't get hit by a stray bullet.

When the bullets and the screaming stop, I hear someone calling my name. I lift my head and look around and jump back as I see a dead John lying a few feet away with his soulless eyes staring back at me.

"Bree!" someone hollers again.

I answer them, but it's too soft, so I try again. "Here… I'm right here."

Two men walk in holding Ar15s. "Are you hurt?"

I shake my head. "No."

One squats down in front of me. "You have a shiner, busted lip… any uh, other injuries…"

I shake my head. "No… but if you had gotten here a second later, I wouldn't be able to say the same. Who are you?"

A bellow from somewhere in the house has me raising up. "Bree!"

"Logan!" I holler back and instantly burst into tears.

I've never seen a man look as afraid as he does. He's taking me in. His jaw clenches as he sees the black eye and busted lip. It's like I can feel the anger pulsing off him, but he's gentle when he reaches for me. "Baby… are you okay?"

He's wiping at my tears, and then I'm dragged against him and he holds me tightly. It's like the last two hours have been a huge emotional roller coaster, and I can't stay strong another second. My knees buckle, and Logan lifts me into his arms.

"Come on. Let's get out of here."

I lean my head against his shoulder and let him carry me out.

We're going out the front of the mansion when Zach steps in front of us. "Lo, you have to put her down. She needs to talk to the detectives. They should be here any minute."

He shakes his head and holds me even tighter. "Zach, look at her. She doesn't need to do anything except go to the hospital."

I put my hand on Logan's chest. "No, I'm fine. I promise. I don't need to go to the hospital. I'll talk to the detectives, and then I want to go home."

He buries his face into my neck and breathes me in. When he lifts his head, he's nodding. "Okay. But if you get tired or—"

I pat his chest. He's devastated. The shock on his face says it all, and that's a lot coming from him. He's the king of keeping his emotions on lockdown.

I pull from his hold, but he doesn't loosen his arms. "Logan, let me down. I'm okay."

He frowns but puts me on my feet. His hand finds mine, and he grips me tightly, pulling me to his side.

I don't know what to make of any of this, but I lean into him.

He looks at Zach. "I want them all dead, Zach. The whole fuckin' Antonelli family. I don't want one of them to think they can retaliate."

Zach shakes his head. "We're not in that business anymore."

Logan opens his mouth, but Zach interrupts him. "I'll talk to Walker. He'll do it legit and the right way. But he'll take care of it."

Logan nods and pulls me to the back of a truck. He sets me on the tailgate and then sits next to me, holding my hand in his.

The detectives come, and I tell them everything that happened tonight. Being in New York, they're familiar with the Antonelli family. Logan stares at me the whole time I'm talking. I can see the pain on his face, but he doesn't say anything. He doesn't have to. The way he's holding me and not letting go says it all.

Finally, when the detectives are done, we're free to go. I ride in the SUV on Logan's lap, and at one point, I fall asleep in his arms.

I wake up when we get to the airfield, but Logan carries me onto the plane and all the way to the back. I'm in and out of sleep. I can hear the murmuring from the guys in the front of the plane, but Logan says nothing. A few times he sends some text messages on his phone, but that's it.

An hour and forty minutes later, we land in Whiskey Run. I try to pull from Logan's arms, but he holds on to me.

I put a hand to his chest. "I want… I need… to walk out of here, Lo."

He searches my eyes and nods. He takes a step back, but before he can get too far, I grab on to his shirt. "But I want you with me."

He covers my hand that is over his heart. "Baby, you can walk out of here, but I'm going to be walking right beside you."

"Thank you," I whisper.

He hugs me to him, kisses my forehead, and then leans back. "You ready?"

I nod, and hand in hand, we walk down the aisle of the plane. All the guys have already gotten off, but they're waiting for us at the bottom of the stairs. I stop at each of the men to thank them. Zach hugs me. "Skyler is worried about you. Please call us if you need anything, okay."

I nod as Logan pulls me back into his arms. He guides me to his waiting truck and calls to Zach, "You need a ride?"

He shakes his head. "No, get her home. I'll catch a ride with one of these guys."

Once we're in the car and driving back toward downtown, I can't help but wonder what's going to happen from here. We haven't talked, but obviously Logan knows some of the story.

I turn in my seat to face him. "Logan, I'm sorry. I did kiss John Antonelli that night, but it didn't mean anything. We were so close to getting them."

He tenses, holding the steering wheel tighter. "I wish you had told me. You were in so much danger, Bree, and—"

I interrupt him. "I know how dangerous it was. That's why I didn't tell you. That's why I never saw you outside of Manhattan. I should have stayed away from you, but I couldn't resist. I wanted to be with you so bad." I suck in a breath. "I'm sorry that I brought all this to you—"

"Stop," he says, almost angry.

I look at Main Street as we pass by. "You missed the turnoff to—"

"You're staying with me."

I tremble, thankful that he's not just taking me home and dropping me off.

"I'm fine with staying at your house, but I don't have any clothes. My phone and my purse are at my apartment."

He's calm and speaks softly. "Aiden and his wife have been blowing up my phone, worried about you. They wanted to do something. I had them bring your phone, purse, toiletries, and clothes to my house."

Shocked, my mouth drops. Logan is always so protective and guarded. "He has access to your house?"

Logan chuckles. "They're your friends. I sent him the code."

I cross my arms over my chest. I have a hundred questions, but I'm not going to ask them now.

We finally get to Logan's house, and he comes around the truck to help me out. His touch is gentle as he walks me up the front stairs. I've driven by his house a few times. I was here before, years ago, but not since I've been back in Whiskey Run.

He disables the alarm and stops when we get inside. He locks the door and resets the alarms. "Come on. I had them put everything in the bedroom."

I follow him, taking in the rooms. Everything is like I remember. Instead of going into the guest bedroom, he goes into his room and flips the light on. I gasp when I see the pile on the bed and the dresser. He looks around. "Your purse and phone are right there," he says, pointing to the dresser. He starts picking up the pile of clothes and carrying them to the closet, hanging them inside. I hold my hands together in front of me. "Uh, I think that's my whole closet."

He answers simply, "It is." He points to the bathroom. "Gracie probably put all your bathroom stuff in there, but if they forgot anything, we will go get it tomorrow."

I look into the adjoining bathroom and see some of my things on the counter. He's walking back and forth from the bed to the closet. "Logan."

"Yeah?" he answers without stopping.

He hangs the last of the clothes, and I take a step toward him. "What is this?"

His eyes lift to mine, and I'm shocked to see his expression. He looks as if he's been punched in the gut or something. He's pale and worried-looking. He doesn't answer my question but walks past me into the bathroom. I follow him as he turns the water on. He holds his hand under the spray, waiting for it to warm up, and when he is satisfied with the temperature, he holds his hand out to me. "Come on. You'll feel better if you shower."

I take a step toward him. "Are you going to shower with me?"

His eyebrows lift. "You want me to?"

I tilt my head to the side. "Yes… can you?"

He nods and reaches for me. Slowly, he lowers to his knee and taps my leg for me to lift my foot. He removes one shoe and sock and then the other. He reaches for the button on my jeans, undoes it, unzips them, and then pulls them down over my thick thighs. He raises to his feet, and I reach for the hem of my shirt, but he takes over, pulling it over my head. When I'm standing in front of him in only a bra and panties, he sucks in a deep breath. He unsnaps my bra and then pulls my panties down my thighs. I step out of them, completely naked. His eyes roam over every bare inch of me, but this look he's giving me is different than normal. It's like he's looking for something, and then it hits me.

"Hey."

His eyes raise to mine, and I point at my face. "This is it. He punched me twice. He didn't… touch me," I tell him.

He bites his lower lip as if he's trying to hold himself together.

I tremble, and he helps me into the shower. I reach for him. "Will you please get in with me?"

He nods and makes quick work of removing his clothes. He doesn't say a word as he steps into the shower. He washes my hair first, and I moan as he massages my scalp. Once he's done there, he moves to my body. My body reacts, nipples erect, but he acts like he's a man on a mission. He's more clinical than anything.

When he's washed all of me, he cleans himself up quickly and turns the water off. His silence is overwhelming. "Lo."

He steps out of the shower and wraps a towel

around his waist. His cock is flaccid, and I'm trying not to take it personally.

He grabs another towel and dries me off. "I'll be right back," he grunts.

He comes back wearing a pair of shorts, and he takes my towel off and pulls one of his T-shirts over my head and down my body.

"Lo… talk to me."

He forces a clenched smile to his face. "I'm going to dry your hair, okay?"

I bite my lip, trying to get a hold of my emotions. "Yeah… yeah, okay."

I keep trying to catch his eyes in the mirror as he dries my hair, but he won't even look at me. It's as if he regrets bringing me here and maybe thinking I'm more trouble than I'm worth.

CHAPTER 19
LOGAN

I grip the hair dryer until my knuckles are white.

I didn't protect her.

I didn't trust her when she said she didn't cheat on me.

I said things to her that I'll regret until my dying day.

Even though I'm feeling all these emotions, I brush through her hair gently, determined that she never feels pain from me again.

I can feel her eyes on me, but I can't look at her. I've never been so ashamed of myself in all my life.

When her hair is dry, I put the blow dryer away and

then finally meet her eyes in the mirror. "Are you hungry? Or do you want to watch—"

She turns to look at me. "I just want to lie down… is that okay?"

"Fuck, honey, that's more than okay."

I pull her gently from the bathroom and turn off the light as we go. I pull the covers down and tuck her into bed. I turn off the light and then walk around to the other side of the bed and lie down next to her.

"Can I hold you?"

I barely get the words out and she throws her body against mine. Instantly, I'm wrapping my arms and my legs around her like I always do. I sigh as she melts into me. My cock twitches, but I do my best to ignore it.

The room is quiet, and Bree whispers my name softly. "Logan."

I stroke my hand down her back. "Yeah, honey?"

Her finger is drawing circles on my chest. "I'm sorry… for everything. For putting you in danger, for putting your family, your friends, your community—"

"Stop," I demand. The fact that she's apologizing to me makes me feel even worse. "Bree… baby… please."

She leans up and looks into my eyes. "I would have never forgiven myself if something had happened to you."

I push her gently to her back and hover over her. I look at her bruised eye and busted lip. "I'm the one that should be apologizing. I should have listened to you, Bree. I should have let you explain—"

She shakes her head. "I did lie to you, Lo. You didn't owe me anything." She huffs out a big breath. "Going against the Antonelli family is not something I wanted to do, but I couldn't say no. I had to—"

I ask her the one question that's been on my mind all night. "Why didn't you tell me? Did you not trust me? Or—"

She puts a finger to my lip. "I trusted you. Heck, I know the kind of man you are. If I had told you, what would you have done?"

I lean toward her. "I wouldn't have left your side."

She nods, not surprised in the least. "Yeah, and that

would have put you in danger. I couldn't—I wouldn't—do that to you."

I shake my head. "You don't get it, do you?"

Her eyebrows lift. "Get what?"

"Baby, I love you—"

She cuts me off. "You mean loved…"

I shake my head. "I mean love. I loved you then and I love you now, Bree. Even when I thought you cheated on me and I wanted to hate you, I couldn't. If something had happened to you—" My voice breaks because just talking about it makes me physically ill.

She cups my cheek. "I feel the same way, Lo. When we broke up, I knew I had to stay in New York for the trial, but as soon as it was over, I came to Whiskey Run. I thought about you every day, and I knew that I had to try. I couldn't lose you. Not like that."

I lean my forehead into hers. "You're the bravest woman I know, honey."

She lifts her shoulders. "I wasn't brave. I was scared to death the whole time."

I clench my eyes closed because I can just imagine how scared she was.

I lift my head and look at her. "It's my turn."

"Your turn for what?"

"My turn to apologize—"

She cuts me off. "No, I get it. You thought I cheated."

I shake my head. "I'm not talking about that. I'm talking about tonight. I wasn't there for you. You were hurt and—"

She puts a hand on each side of my face. "That wasn't your fault, Lo. And you and your men came to get me."

Almost fiercely, I tell her, "I will always come to get you. I promise you that from this moment, I will be by your side. I will stand by you and protect you and—"

She juts her chin at me. "For how long? Nine months?"

I shake my head adamantly. "Forever, Bree. You're mine."

Her eyes widen, and she winces as if it's painful. I lean down and kiss her cheek softly. "You need to rest, baby. We can talk in the morning."

Her hands go to my shoulders. "I don't want to rest, Logan. I'm numb… and I just want to feel something."

I tilt my head. "Feel something?"

She slides her hand down my stomach. "Yeah, I want to get lost in you. I don't want to think about these last two years without you. I want—"

"Baby… are you sure? You've been through a traumatic—"

She cuts me off and cups my manhood. "Yes, I'm sure. I want you."

My hips jerk, pushing against her hold. I rest my forehead to hers. "I don't want to hurt you."

She pushes me to my back. She pulls down my shorts while I lift my hips. In one movement, she sits astride me and pulls the T-shirt she's wearing up her body and then throws it across the room.

Her hands go to my chest, and she smiles softly at me. "What do you think? You game?"

My hands go to her hips. "I just don't want to hurt you… I'll never hurt you again, Bree."

I hold back, not wanting to push myself on her, needing to know she's okay.

She slides backwards, and my cock twitches against her ass.

She squirms on me and then leans up so she can wrap her hand around my girth.

I suck in a breath as she lines me up to her center and slowly impales herself on me. I lean up, unable to hold back any longer. Pressing our chests together, I hold her to me. She starts to move, riding me, squeezing me until I feel that I'm going to explode.

She moans, and not wanting to hurt her cut lip, I kiss her neck.

She leans back, and I suckle her breast as she rides me.

"Yes," she moans.

I lift my hips, meeting her thrust for thrust. She circles her hips, grinding her clit against me. Her moans get louder, and her pussy gets wetter. "Don't stop," she begs. I wrap my arms around her, holding tightly so that I can punch my hips against her.

Her release sets me off, and we both moan as our orgasms take over.

I fill her up, releasing my seed deep inside her, and when she falls limp in my arms, I lean back, turning her so she's lying on her back.

I look down into her hooded eyes. "I'll be right back."

She holds on to me. "No… please don't go."

I nip at her lip. "I'm going to get us cleaned up, and then I'm coming back to bed… okay?"

She's scared and rightfully so. She's been through a lot, not just tonight but for the last two years. Knowing what I know now, I'm assuming that since she moved here to Whiskey Run, she's been looking over her shoulder every second.

In this moment, I vow she won't have to do that anymore. I'm going to take care of her. She won't have anything to worry about.

I clean myself up and then carry a warm cloth back to the bedroom. I push Bree's knees apart, and she holds her hand out. "I can do it."

I hold the towel out of her reach. "I want to do it."

She must see the determination in my eyes because she doesn't argue with me any further. I clean her up, toss the towel into the hamper, and then lie down next to her. I don't have to say anything; she just leans into me, wrapping herself around me. She melts into me and sighs.

"I love you," I whisper.

I can feel her smile against my chest. "I love you, too."

CHAPTER 20
BREE

I wake up with the sun shining through the drapes. I stretch, and then all of a sudden, last night comes to mind, and I shoot up in bed. The room is empty, and I barely hold back the scream for Logan.

My heart is racing.

I break out in a sweat and have to talk myself down. *I'm okay. I'm in Logan's house, and he's here somewhere.*

I get up and grab the T-shirt I wore to bed last night. I pull it over my head and down my body and then walk into the bathroom. The room is filled with steam, and it brings me some comfort to smell Logan's signature scent.

I look at myself in the mirror, wincing when I see my swollen eye and lip. I smile and make different movements. At least it doesn't feel as bad as it looks, I guess.

I freshen up quickly and then walk through the house, finding Logan standing in the kitchen at the stove with his back to me. I just stand here, staring at his bare back, watching his muscles pull as he cooks.

"Morning," he says before turning around.

He frowns when he sees my bruises. He walks over to me and gently cups my face in his hands. "I love you."

I put my hands to his bare chest. "I love you too, Logan. But we should talk."

He frowns at that. "Fine, but you have to eat first."

He plates the food and carries it over to the table. I follow behind him, not wanting to tell him that I'm not hungry.

I sit down in front of the plate of eggs, bacon, and toast. It looks good, and I put some eggs on my fork and take a bite since Logan's staring at me expectantly. He nods approvingly, then walks back over to the stove to prepare his plate.

I take a few more bites, and he brings over cups of orange juice and finally sits down with me.

We eat in silence for a few minutes, and when I don't think I can eat another bite, I set my fork down. "Logan…"

He follows my lead and sets his fork down. "Yeah?"

I clench my hands together on the table. "I think we should talk about… everything."

He tilts his head to the side. "Everything? What does that mean?"

I take a deep breath. "I mean I feel like everything is happening so fast, and we need to slow down."

He tenses and sits up a little taller. He clears his throat, and his voice is almost strangled. "What does that mean… slow down?"

I throw my hands up. "I mean before yesterday we were fuck buddies and you hated me, and last night you're saying that we're going to be together."

He sucks in a breath and stares at me intensely. "Do you love me?"

I shake my head. "That's not the point."

He reaches for my hands and holds both them in his. "Do. You. Love. Me?"

I roll my eyes. "You know I do."

"Then if you want to slow down because you need time, that's fine. I'll wait for as long as you want me to. But all the waiting will be with me by your side."

I pull my hands from his and put my palms flat on the table. I need to explain this, and I can't do it with him touching me. "Lo, I want you to be with me because you love me, not because you feel guilty or—"

"Feel guilty!" he exclaims. He shoots to his feet. "Stay right here."

I watch him walk out of the room, and I push my plate farther away. I fidget in my seat, wondering what he's doing and secretly praying that he doesn't let me push him away.

I want to do what's right, but I don't know if he's going to let me.

He comes back into the kitchen and stops, staring down at me. "Bree—"

I look down at my hands. "Logan, this is hard

enough as it is. I want to be with you, but I want you to choose me—"

He gets down on one knee in front of me. "I do choose you. I will always choose you."

I search his eyes, and all I see is the sincerity shining from him. He grabs my hand, and it's then I see the box he's carrying. He opens it, takes a ring out, and sets the box down on the table. "I've had this ring since our third date. I knew then that I wanted to marry you." He shrugs. "And yeah, we weren't together for the last two years, but I can honestly say that I thought about you and missed you every day. Bree, you make my life so much better. Hell, you make me happy—fuck, happier than I've ever been."

He shudders a breath. "So yeah, if you want to take it slow because you're not sure, then we'll take it slow. But just know that as soon as you're ready, I have this ring, and I'm waiting for you."

I bite my lip to hold back my emotions. I want to tell him that I don't have any doubts and I don't need any time, but before I can get it out, he continues, leaning toward me. "But just know that I'm hoping you decide you want to be with me soon, because I want to start a family with you, and I'm ready now."

My heart flips in my chest. "You want..." I can't even get the words out.

He nods his head. "Yes, I know I'm not the most romantic-talking guy, so I'm just going to say it how I feel. I want my ring on your finger. I want my baby in your belly. I want to go to sleep with you in my bed next to me. I want to wake up with you beside me every morning."

I gasp as if I'm just now realizing the truth. "You really do love me, don't you?"

He chuckles. "More than anything, baby. I love you more than anything."

I lift my chin to him. "Ask me."

His eyes widen, but he doesn't waste any time. He holds the beautiful diamond ring up to me. "Bree Banks, will you please do me the honor of being my wife? Please...make me the happiest man on Earth."

I let out a sob. "Yes, yes, I'll marry you."

He slides the ring on my finger, and I glance at the

sparkling diamond and then back into his big brown eyes. "I love you, Logan Brody."

He stands up, pulling me with him. "I love you too, Bree, soon to be Brody."

Gently, he kisses me, avoiding the cut on my lip.

I'm sobbing as he pulls away. He's wiping at my tears, and a look of worry fills his face. "What is this? Don't cry. I can't stand it when you cry, baby."

I sniffle, trying to rein it in. "I'm just so happy. More than anything, I wanted to be with you, and I just can't believe"—I suck in a shuddered breath—"you're making all my dreams come true, Lo."

He nods and looks at me solemnly. "And from this point forward, that's what I'm going to do. I'm going to give you everything you want."

I lean into him. "You… that's all I want." I can't stop the smile from forming on my face. "And a baby. I want one of those too."

He groans. "Fuck, just thinking about it makes me crazy."

I blink wide-eyed at him. "So… we're getting married… and we're having a baby."

He holds me to him, burying his face into my neck, kissing me. "Yes and I'm thinking sooner rather than later."

I loop my arms around his neck. "Okay. Whenever."

He jerks back. "Whenever?" He grips my upper arms. "Don't say that unless you mean it."

I shrug. "I do mean it. I want to marry you, Lo. I don't want to wait."

His voice is husky and filled with emotion. "You don't want to wait? I'm sure you've had dreams about your wedding."

I shake my head. "Nope. As long as you're who I'm marrying, that's all I need."

He tenses up and asks softly, "So if we had a wedding in say, two weeks, you'd do it? You'd marry me?"

I nod and tell him truthfully, "I would marry you today."

He stares into my eyes. "Two weeks from today. We're getting married."

He's looking at me like I'm going to change my mind or something. "Okay."

He pulls me to him. "Bree, I'm not joking. We're getting married in two weeks."

I smile and cup his face with my hands. "Logan Brody, I can't wait."

He scoops me up in his arms and swings me around. I'm laughing when he stops spinning and starts carrying me down the hall.

"We should probably celebrate."

I nod as he puts me on my feet next to the bed. I pull the T-shirt I'm wearing off my body. "Yeah, we should definitely celebrate."

He pulls his shorts down and kicks them off his legs. I don't even wait for him to ask; I jump into his arms, and my legs go around his waist.

He holds me like he never wants to let me go.

Together, we fall onto the bed. We're both where we're meant to be, and we're ready for a future that is ours.

CHAPTER 21
LOGAN

I pull at my collar and look around the church.

My brother Miller whispers to me, "You okay?"

I turn to look at him. "Where is she?"

He laughs and looks at his watch. "We still have fifteen minutes before the ceremony even starts."

I look around at the small crowd. We invited our family, but half of them are standing up beside me. My sister is somewhere in the church with my soon-to-be bride, and I'm getting impatient. I start walking down the aisle, and my mom stops me. "Honey, where are you going?"

I look at her and my dad. They're both tan and happy-looking. They've been on several cruises over the last few months, but they cut their trip short to come home for my wedding. "I'm going to get my bride."

I lean down and kiss Mom's cheek and then hug my dad. With a determined stride, I walk to the back of the church and listen for my fiancée. I hear my sister talking, and I follow her voice. When I get to the door where they're at, I knock loudly.

Their talking stops, but no one answers the door.

"Bree!" I demand.

I can hear her walk to the door, but she doesn't open it. "Logan… what are you doing?"

Half-frustrated, I ask, "What are you doing?"

She giggles. "Uh, I'm getting ready for our wedding."

I lean my forehead against the wood door. "Well, are you almost done?"

Slowly, the door opens, and I raise up. I'm not the least bit prepared for the vision in front of me. "Bree…" I breathe.

She smiles widely at me. "Logan."

She pulls the door open wider, and I look at her. She's wearing a form-fitting white dress, her hair is flowing down her shoulders, and her lips are painted a pretty pink. She literally takes my breath away. "You're so beautiful."

She leans against the doorway. "You're pretty handsome yourself."

My sister comes toward us. "Okay, well, now that I can see she's taken care of, I'm going to go and let everyone know we're starting early."

I just nod, and Bree thanks my sister.

"So we're doing this," Bree says.

I nod, staring at her because I can't get enough. "I don't want to wait another second to start my life with you."

I lean down to kiss her, and she leans into me. I deepen the kiss, and when she moans, I reluctantly break it off. "Are you ready?"

She nods, and I smooth my thumb across her lip. "I messed up your lipstick."

She shrugs. "It's okay. I have a feeling you're just going to smudge it again."

I laugh. "Guaranteed."

I hold my hand out to her, and she puts hers in it. I thread our fingers together. "You ready?"

She leans her head back to look up at me. "Am I ready to spend the rest of my life with the love of my life?"

I bring her hand up between us and kiss her knuckles, and she leans into me. "Yeah, I'm ready."

I pull her through the church, and she's huffing as we get to the aisle. "Are we in a hurry?"

I nod my head. "Yeah, I need my ring on your finger."

She laughs and pats my chest. "Oh, Logan. Don't you know? I don't need a ring or a piece of paper. I have been yours since the first day I laid eyes on you in that bodega."

"Same," I say as I lean down and kiss her.

I gesture to the other end of the aisle. My sister, Skyler, and all my brothers are standing up there next to the pastor. They're all beaming at us, and I couldn't stop smiling even if I tried.

Hand in hand, we walk down the aisle, ready to make it official. She's mine, and I'm hers. And together, we can build the life we've always dreamed of.

EPILOGUE

BREE

Three Months Later

I've been laughing so hard that my cheeks are hurting. Seeing Logan with all his siblings is, well, pure chaos. They're always picking on each other and giving each other crap, but in it all, it's easy to see that they all love each other.

Guy and Ozzy are in the corner playing cards. I know that they're either talking about ranching or baseball because they talk about that a lot.

Miller is on his phone looking grumpy again.

Penn is even here today with Aria, even though they seem to be avoiding each other.

Zach is over at the grill with Logan and Sky, and Aria and I are doing some last-minute touchups on side dishes.

"So… how is it being married to my brother?" Skyler holds her hands up. "No returns, so if you've changed your mind—"

She's smiling ear to ear, teasing me, and I laugh, deciding that I'll tease her right back. "Oh, you want to know what it's like being married to Logan? Well, last night we…" I pause and wiggle my eyebrows at her.

She scrunches up her nose. "No, absolutely not. Do not say another word. I don't want to hear about my brother…" She starts making gagging noises just as Zach walks in, and he comes at her with concern etched on his face. "Oh no, baby, are you all right?"

He puts a hand to her belly. Skyler is only a few months pregnant, but that doesn't faze Zach. He doesn't let her lift a finger.

She covers his hand with hers. "No, this time it wasn't your baby… it was my sister-in-law trying to tell me about—ugh, I can't even say."

I just giggle at her theatrics.

Logan is manning the grill, and even though he's only a few feet away, I miss him.

I grab a cold beer and let Aria and Skyler know I'll be right back. I walk toward him, and I love the way he looks me up and down as I approach. "Here you go."

He wraps an arm around me and pulls me to him as he takes the beer. "Baby, you just brought me one not five minutes ago. Are you missing me? Or trying to get me drunk so you can take advantage of me later?"

Instead of answering him, I shrug with the biggest smile on my face.

He leans in, kisses my neck, and whispers into my ear, "As soon as I get rid of all these people, I'm going to show you how much I've missed you."

I blurt out a laugh. "Oh, you miss me? You do know we made love not an hour ago."

He shakes his head. "Too long."

I roll my eyes, and Skyler giggling has me looking toward her and Zach. I sigh, not trying to hide my jealousy. "Your sister is glowing with her pregnancy."

Logan snuggles into me. "It's been three months, baby. We're just getting started."

I sigh. "I know, I just, I don't know. If you want three kids... we sort of need to get started."

He hugs me to him, and I know he wants to protect me from my own feelings. "Baby, this just means I get more time with you to myself. We'll have however many kids we're supposed to have."

I nod, wanting to believe what he's saying. He seems so sure of everything that it brings me comfort too.

I kiss him softly. "I love you, husband."

He tries to deepen the kiss. "I love you too, wife."

I giggle and pull away, shyly looking around at our family. "Your whole family is here."

He rubs his thumb over my swollen lip. "You mean our family."

I nod, and Aria catches my eye. She's watching Penn with a frown on her face as he types into his phone. I've wanted to ask her if she's okay, but she's pretty tight-lipped about everything with her and her husband. I've asked Logan, but he doesn't know either. I can only imagine how stressful it is with

Penn being a doctor. And I'm sure Aria is stressed working and taking care of the home. I mentally make a note to ask her to lunch soon.

Miller walks up to us, and for once the frown is gone, and he has a soft smile on his face. He doesn't say anything, just smiles as he looks between Logan and me.

"What is it?" Logan asks him.

He just shrugs. "Nothing." He takes a deep breath and then starts to ramble. "I mean, you all are really happy, aren't you?"

I look at Logan, and I know the love I see in his eyes is reflected in my own. I nod at Miller. "Yeah, we are."

He crosses his arms over his chest. "Yeah, well, I'm glad you two found each other. Some people spend years wanting something they can't have.

My eyebrows lift with curiosity. I don't think he thought his statement would be so honest and vulnerable. It's hard to imagine that Miller of all people has experienced unrequited love. He blushes, but before either of us can say anything, his phone rings.

He looks at it and then gets a soft smile on his face.

Without saying a word to us, he walks off to the side, and we can't help but hear part of his conversation. "Hey."

He pauses and then says, "No, I told you to call me if you ever needed me. Tell me where you are."

He stands up a little taller. "I'm on my way." He walks over to us. "Sorry. I gotta go."

Logan asks him, "Is everything okay?"

He nods. "Yeah. Everything's okay. Or it's going to be. Just something I've been waiting on."

He strides through the family, bidding everyone goodbye, leaving Logan and me wondering about the mysterious call.

Logan pulls me to him and kisses my forehead. "You know, I'm glad we found each other too. That day I walked into the bodega, I knew as soon as I looked at you that my life would never be the same."

In his arms, I feel how right he is. "My life is not the same either, but this is exactly what I wanted."

He smiles happily. "Me too."

EPILOGUE 2

LOGAN

Six Years Later

"Honey, I'm home."

I walk through the quiet house and am surprised at the silence. It doesn't feel right.

I keep walking, a smile on my face, ready to see my wife and kids. I know they're here somewhere. I talked to Bree not twenty minutes ago.

I walk into the kitchen and find it empty. One peek out the window and my eyes are drawn to my wife and kids in the pool.

Instead of going outside, I sneak upstairs, take off my clothes, put on some swimming trunks, and then walk out to join my family.

The three kids start whooping and hollering when they see me. My beautiful wife stays in the pool as the kids clamor out and run for me.

I happily hug each of them and then toss them into the pool. They're all giggles and laughter, and before I realize it, I've started something. For the next twenty minutes, I'm tossing kids into the pool. They land in the water and then rush to get out to do it again. Bree has her sunglasses on, but I can feel her gaze on me. She's smiling and laughing. "You see what you started?"

I laugh. "How was your day?" I ask her.

She smiles. "It was a good day. Last days of summer. They're excited about school starting on Monday."

"Hey, you guys. What do you think about having a carpet picnic tonight, and we'll watch one of your favorite movies."

"Yes!" they all scream in unison.

I jump into the pool with them. Bridget jumps on my back, Britney loops her arms around my neck, and Braxton is treading water in front of me. They are each talking about which movie we should watch. I'm only a few feet away from Bree, but I need to touch her. "All right, I got an idea. One of you pick what we're having for dinner, one of you pick the first movie, and one of you pick the second movie."

"Yes!" they scream.

I laugh. "Okay, but you know the drill. Showers first."

They're so excited that they get out of the pool and start drying off. Bree starts to get out, but I hold her to me. "Oh no, where do you think you're going?"

She doesn't resist. She curls into me. "You do know you're sending three wet five-year-olds into the house. They're going to destroy the floors."

I hold her to me. "I'll clean them."

She loops her arms around my neck. "Mr. Brody, did you just manipulate our kids to get me alone?"

I have no qualms about telling her the truth. "I did."

She puts one hand on my chest, twirling her finger across my skin. "And the carpet picnic with two movies... you know they'll fall asleep in the first one."

I chuckle. "I know. And then I'll have some alone time with my wife."

She leans into me. "I've missed you."

I lean down and kiss her until we're both breathless. My cock reacts to her, and there's no concealing it. "Fuck, I need you."

She looks into my eyes. "I need you too."

With a groan, I rest my forehead against hers. "I don't know if I'll be able to make it to that second movie without touching you."

She laughs but is quiet.

"You okay?" I ask her.

Bree wanted to stay home with the kids, and now that they'll be going back to school, she's planning to go back to work a few days a week. I have tried not to pressure her. I wanted it to be her decision, but we definitely miss her at the office.

She shrugs, and I get worried.

"You know, if you don't want to go back to work—"

She shakes her head. "It's not that."

I put my hand on her chin and tilt her head so she has to look at me. "What is it then?"

She shrugs. "Are you happy, Lo? I mean, with me?"

Stunned, I just stare at her. "Am I happy with you?"

She nods. "Yeah, I mean we said three kids, but we never dreamed we'd have triplets. Our house, our lives, it's like… I dunno, constant chaos."

I laugh and then realize she's serious. "Sweetie, I don't think you get it. I grew up with five brothers and one sister. That was chaos and craziness, but I wouldn't have changed a second of it. This is exactly what I wanted. I'd choose you and our kids a thousand times."

She smiles at me as if a weight has been lifted off her shoulders. She must have really been worried about this. I need to up my game. I never want her to feel like I don't want this life.

I pull her hair back off her shoulders and kiss her neck. "What about you? Are you happy?"

She nods and tilts her head so I can have better access to her neck. "Yeah, I'm happy. Happy with you, the kids. I mean, I would have liked to have kept my body but—"

I cut her off. "Your body is perfect."

She blurts out a laugh. "Logan, it's fine. I wasn't fishing for compliments. I had triplets. I know I don't look like I used to—"

I shake my head sternly. "Oh no, don't do that. Bree, baby, this body kept our babies safe until they were ready to be born, and then this body nourished them. This body is strength, love, and sacrifice. It's perfect… you're perfect."

I grip her ass and pull her to me. Instantly, she lifts her legs and wraps them around my waist. She wraps herself around me and rests her head on my shoulder. "Yeah, that second movie was a good idea, Lo."

I chuckle. "Yeah, now I have to figure out how to get out of this pool without three little sets of eyes seeing me."

She slides her body along mine, and my cock twitches in my shorts. "You're not helping matters," I tell her.

She doesn't stop, though. "I know… I just need…"

She doesn't finish, but I know what she needs. I look over her head, and Britney is coming out the door. "Okay, we got it figured out. I'm picking the food, and I pick pizza. Braxton is picking the first movie, and Bridget is picking the second movie."

My voice is calmer than I feel. "Great job, honey. Have you three showered?"

She shakes her head. "No, Dad, we were figuring out who was doing what."

I nod. "Okay, good thinking. Now that it's all planned out, you get in Mom and Dad's shower, Bridget gets in the hallway shower, and tell Braxton to get in the downstairs shower. We'll be inside in fifteen minutes, and then we'll get the night started."

She disappears into the house, and instantly, I have my hand in the bottoms of my wife's bathing suit.

She jerks. "Logan… we can't…"

I chuckle. "Baby, you're so fuckin' close already… let me just take the edge off."

I stroke my finger through her folds and then caress her swollen clit. She comes in an instant, like I knew she would. She's biting her lip to stop from screaming out.

I hold on to her as the tremors wrack through her.

When she's coming down, she slides her hand down my body and cups me through my shorts. "What about you?"

I grab her wrist. "I'll wait until I can have you naked underneath me."

She sighs as I carry her out of the pool. "You're a good man, Logan Brody."

I kiss her again. "I'm good because you make me want to be a better man. I love you, Bree."

She slips her hand into mine, and we walk into our chaotic, love-filled home.

ALSO BY HOPE FORD

Want more of Whiskey Run?

Whiskey Run

Faithful - He's the hot, say-it-like-it-is cowboy, and he won't stop until he gets the woman he wants.

Captivated - She's a beautiful woman on the run... and I'm going to be the one to keep her.

Obsessed - She's loved him since high school and now he's back.

Seduced - He's a football player that falls in love with the small town girl.

Devoted - She's a plus size model and he's a small town mechanic.

Whiskey Run: Savage Ink

Virile - He won't let her go until he puts his mark on her.

Torrid - He'll do anything to give her what she wants.

Rigid - If you love reading about emotionally wounded men and the women that help them overcome their past, then you'll love Dawson and Emily's story.

Whiskey Run: Cowboys Love Curves

Obsessed Cowboy - She's the preacher's daughter and she's off limits.

Whiskey Run: Heroes

Ransom - He's on a mission he can't lose.

Redeem - He's in love with his sister's best friend.

Submit - She's his fake wife but he wants to make it real.

Forbid - They have a secret romance but he's about to stake his claim.

Whiskey Run: Sugar

One Night Love - Her one night stand wants more.

Rebound Love - She's falling for the rebound guy.

Second Chance Love - He is not a man to ignore... especially when he asks for a second chance.

Bad Boy Love - He's a bad boy that wants her good.

Whiskey Run: Guardians MC

Protective Biker - She needs his protection and he'll give it to her. But he's going to need her heart in exchange.

Broken Biker - There's only one woman for him…

Relentless Biker - He won't stop until he has her back.

Whiskey Men

Reluctant Husband - If you love reading about curvy women getting the hot guy, opposites attract, jealousy trope, marriage of convenience, and small-town romance, then you'll love Lucas and Isabella's story.

Something Real - If you love reading billionaire, single father, age gap, boss/employee, and small-town romance, then you'll love Ford and Lilian's story.

Coming Home - If you love reading billionaire, ex-military, age gap, forced proximity, and small-town romance, then you'll love Hudson and Elle's story.

Forever Mine - If you love reading billionaire, age gap, second chance, and small-town romance, then you'll love Beau and Natalie's story.

Always Yours - If you love reading billionaire, friends to lovers, pregnancy, and small town romance, then you'll love Austin and Ally's story.

JOIN ME!

JOIN MY NEWSLETTER

www.AuthorHopeFord.com/Subscribe

BE A HOTTIE!

JOIN HOPE'S HOTTIES ON FACEBOOK

www.FB.com/groups/hopeford

A place to talk about Hope Ford's books! Find out about new releases, giveaways, get exclusive content, see covers before anyone else and more!

ABOUT THE AUTHOR

USA Today Bestselling Author Hope Ford writes short, steamy, sweet romances. She loves tattooed, alpha men, instant love stories, and ALWAYS happily ever afters.

To find me on Pinterest, Instagram, Facebook, Goodreads, and more:

www.AuthorHopeFord.com/follow-me

Want FREE BOOKS?
Go to www.authorhopeford.com/freebies

www.ingramcontent.com/pod-product-compliance
Lightning Source LLC
Chambersburg PA
CBHW020032310726
48970CB00007B/2221